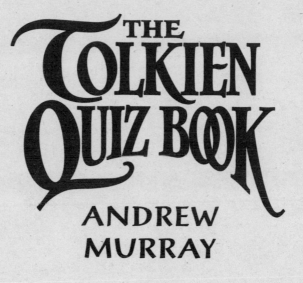

THE TOLKIEN QUIZ BOOK

ANDREW MURRAY

D0097301

HarperCollins*Publishers*

PREFACE

The otherness, grandeur and heroic scope of J. R. R. Tolkien's Middle-earth seem to have filled a void in so many modern lives that it's rare to find someone who doesn't at least know that *The Hobbit* has a dragon in it somewhere and that *The Lord of the Rings* is the first really fat book young teenagers like to read and re-read again and again. Professor Tolkien is one of that select band of writers who can claim to have almost single-handedly created a literary genre and has carved himself such a distinctive niche in mainstream culture that there are plenty who haven't read a word of his books but *know* they don't like them.

Perhaps you have just second-hand impressions of the world of Bilbo, Gandalf and the Ring through friends' enthusiasms, in which case the Starter question in each section is there to help ease you into the subject – after that, you're probably on your own, with only your friends' knowing smiles to taunt you for every mis-pronunciation and missed accent. Don't worry – there are plenty of tough ones with which to get your own back (and no, you must be joking, *I* couldn't answer all of these if I were put on the spot). And, while the Starters are generally easier than the main questions, the Tie-breakers are not necessarily harder but are there for when the competition gets nail-bitingly close.

The questions are drawn not only from the Middle-earth canon but from the short stories *Smith of Wootton Major*, *Farmer Giles of Ham* and *Leaf by Niggle*, and from biographical material. If you haven't yet explored the delights of these peripheral lands, I hope that the questions will encourage you to pack your rucksack and lose yourself in Tolkien's world – it's so preferable to our own. It's also a world, thank goodness, enjoyed by millions outside that young teenage clique, and the older you get, the more you come to love the richness of Tolkien's creations.

Andrew Murray, 1996

CONTENTS

HarperCollins*Publishers*
77–85 Fulham Palace Road
Hammersmith, London w6 8jb

First published by
HarperCollins*Publishers* 1996
9 8 7 6 5 4 3 2 1

ISBN 0 261 10346 6

Printed in Great Britain by Caledonian
International Book Manufacturing Ltd,
Glasgow

QUESTIONS:

1 · LET THERE BE LIGHT

STARTER

◆ Who gave Bilbo Baggins riddles in the dark?

1 What were Illuin and Ormal?

2 Which respective Maiar guided the Sun and the Moon?

3 What were collected in the Wells of Varda?

4 How did Sam pass the Two Watchers of Cirith Ungol?

5 Who did Frodo see in a dream with the Moon shining in his hair?

6 What did the setting sun of Durin's Day reveal to Bilbo?

7 Who sailed the heavens with a Silmaril upon his brow?

8 Who was the Lady of the Stars?

9 Who were the Moriquendi?

10 Where was the Rath Celerdain, and what did it mean?

TIE BREAK

◆ What city stood in the Calacirya, the Pass of Light?

2 · CONCERNING HOBBITS

STARTER

◆ How many Hobbits joined the Fellowship of the Ring?

1 Who was Bilbo Baggins' mother?

2 According to Hobbit records, who were the only hobbits to surpass Bullroarer in height?

3 Name the three strains of hobbits.

4 Who first cultivated Pipe-weed?

5 By what name were hobbits known in the Grey-elven tongue?

6 Which hobbit first discovered the One Ring?

7 Where were hobbits said to have lived before they settled in the Shire?

8 What colours were hobbits notably fond of?

9 Which hobbit-clan had a reputation for adventurousness even before Bilbo's adventures?

10 Which famous hobbit compiled the '*Herblore of the Shire*', the '*Reckoning of Years*' and the treatise '*Old Words and Names in the Shire*'?

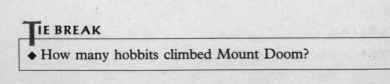

TIE BREAK

◆ How many hobbits climbed Mount Doom?

3 · BILBO BAGGINS

◆ What was the name of Bilbo's home?

1 Who was Bilbo's maternal grandfather?

2 What phrase did he use for a lot of things?

3 At what time was Bilbo expected to be at the 'Green Dragon'?

4 What couldn't Bilbo do any more than fly like a bat?

5 How did Bilbo know that Sting was an Elvish blade?

6 What did he mean to say when he squealed 'Time! Time!'?

7 What did Bilbo spot on the far bank of the black stream?

8 Who did he give the Arkenstone to?

9 What did Bilbo find was going on when he arrived home?

10 What major work of scholarship did Bilbo produce in Rivendell?

TIE BREAK

◆ Where was Bilbo heading when he passed the Old Took's record for longevity?

4 · NUMBERS

STARTER

◆ 'Three Rings for the Elven-kings under the sky...' How many rings are mentioned in this verse?

1 How old was Bilbo when he gave his farewell birthday party?

2 How many Black Riders assailed Frodo and his companions on Weathertop?

3 How many dogs did Frodo and his companions encounter at Farmer Maggot's farm, and what were their names?

4 Which three dwarves, formerly of Thorin's company, are mentioned among those who disappeared into the darkness of Moria?

5 How many Valar were there?

6 Who had seven toes upon each foot?

7 What number was Denethor II in the line of the Stewards of Gondor?

8 Who sang about fifteen birds in five firtrees?

9 How many gates blocked the mighty ravine of Orfalch Echor?

10 Where did Elendil and his sons keep the seven palantíri?

TIE BREAK

◆ What does Nirnaeth Arnoediad mean?

5 · THE SHIRE

STARTER

◆ What kind of people were the main inhabitants of the Shire?

1 What river marked the eastern boundary of the Shire?

2 What stone marked the centre of the Shire?

3 What had been the only battle fought within the borders of the Shire before the War of the Ring?

4 What was the chief township of the Shire?

5 Into how many Farthings was the Shire divided?

6 Name four inns in the Shire.

7 What township lay on the other side of Bag End from Hobbiton?

8 What happened when the river Brandywine froze over in the Fell Winter?

9 To which family had the office of Thain fallen?

10 What officials acted as the police of the Shire?

TIE BREAK

◆ What was the last battle fought in the Shire?

6 · THERE...

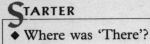

STARTER

◆ Where was 'There'?

1 What did Bilbo twice ask Gandalf for?

2 Who played on a golden harp at the Unexpected Party?

3 Who always acted as look-out for Thorin's Company?

4 Where did Bilbo discover Sting?

5 What did Elrond discover about the Company's map?

6 What did Bilbo lose as he escaped from the Misty Mountains?

7 How did Dori help Bilbo to escape from the Wargs?

8 Why had the Wargs come to the same glade as Thorin's Company?

9 What was most remarkable about Beorn?

10 How did Bilbo and the dwarves escape from the Elvenking's palace?

TIE BREAK

◆ Who did Bilbo ask, 'Well, are you alive or are you dead'?

7 ...AND BACK AGAIN

STARTER

◆ What town stood on stilts on the Long Lake?

1 How did the people of Lake-town react to the arrival of Thorin?

2 What river flowed out of the Lonely Mountain and into the Long Lake?

3 What time of the year was it when the Company reached the Lonely Mountain?

4 What happened when the great thrush knocked on the stone?

5 What did Bilbo first steal from the dragon-hoard?

6 How was Bard able to kill Smaug, and who gave him the necessary advice?

7 What kind of creature was Roäc, and who was his father?

8 What was the name of the Goblin chief at the Battle of Five Armies?

9 Who became King under the Mountain after Thorin's death?

10 Which two friends came to visit Bilbo at Bag End?

TIE BREAK

◆ Whose lullaby, said Bilbo, 'would waken a drunken goblin'?

8 · WHO SAID...? – 1

◆ Who flattered Smaug on his 'waistcoat of fine diamonds'?

Who said the following:

1 'You! You! You miserable hobbit! You undersized – burglar!'

2 'What a lot of things you do use '*Good morning*' for!'

3 'This shall be my own kingdom; and I name it unto myself!'

4 'This is the One Ring that he lost many ages ago, to the great weakening of his power. He greatly desires it – but he must *not* get it.'

5 'What have I got in my pocket?'

6 'Almost felt you liked the Forest! That's good! That's uncommonly kind of you.'

7 'You have nice manners for a thief and a liar.'

8 'If I was after the Ring, I could have it – NOW!'

9 'I have it! Of course, of course! Absurdly simple, like most riddles when you see the answer.'

10 'Well, I'm back.'

TIE BREAK

◆ Who told Ar-Pharazôn that Melkor was 'Lord of All' and 'Giver of Freedom'?

9 · THE MISTY MOUNTAINS

◆ Did the Misty Mountains run North-South or East-West?

1 By what Sindarin name were the Misty Mountains also known?

2 Which dwarves were sent by Thorin's Company to find a cave to shelter in?

3 Which dwarf carried Bilbo on his back as they escaped from the mountain goblins?

4 Which high peak marked the extreme north-western limit of the Misty Mountains?

5 Which ruler of men, whose kingdom bordered on the Misty Mountains, was to become one of Sauron's most trusted servants?

6 In the Elvish tongue, what were the names of the three tall peaks that stood over Moria?

7 By what name was the Dimrill Dale known to the Dwarves, and what did they call the mere that lay in it?

8 What sort of trees flanked the West-door of Moria?

9 What river flowed from the Dimrill Dale through Lórien to the River Anduin?

10 The Gap of Rohan separated the Misty Mountains from what other mountain range?

TIE BREAK

◆ Which of these peaks was not in the Misty Mountains: Dolmed, Gundabad, Barazinbar, Methedras?

10 · DWARVES

◆ Did Dwarves prefer trees, stone or the Sea?

1 Who created the Seven Fathers of the Dwarves?

2 What were the three Dwarf-realms mentioned in Elven histories, and under what mountain ranges had they been delved?

3 Who called the Dwarves 'Gonnhirrim' and what did it mean?

4 Who was the greatest of all Dwarf smiths?

5 What mansion did the Dwarves build for King Thingol?

6 What was the Nauglamír, and who did the Dwarves make it for?

7 Who became the first King under the Mountain in Erebor?

8 What great battle was fought between Dwarves and Orcs at Moria's East-gate?

9 Which King under the Mountain fell with King Brand of Dale in the War of the Ring?

10 Which Dwarf was called Elf-friend and what is claimed to have been his final, unique destiny?

TIE BREAK

◆ Which race of Elves were the Dwarves closest to?

11 · TOLKIEN CARTOGRAPHY

STARTER

◆ What kind of light revealed secrets on Thorin's map?

1 Name the large expanse of water in Southern Mordor.

2 What island lay near the mouth of the River Anduin?

3 Where was the Northern end of the Greenway?

4 What mountain range marked the Western boundary of Mordor?

5 Which river joined the Anduin between the Falls of Rauros and Cair Andros?

6 What realm was flanked by the Misty Mountains to the East and the Ettenmoors to the South?

7 What great peak stood on the Western side of Minas Tirith?

8 What river flowed down to the Grey Havens?

9 What hills lay to the East of Erebor?

10 What was the name of the kingdom of Thingol and Melian?

TIE BREAK

◆ What dwelling did Turgon build in the region of Nevrast?

12 · FLORA AND FAUNA

STARTER

◆ What were the trolls cooking when Bilbo and Company found them?

1 Who slew the great boar of Everholt but died in the process?

2 What was the name of Oromë's steed?

3 By what other name was the plant *athelas* known, and what was its chief virtue?

4 Name the five ponies that were *stolen* from the stables of 'The Prancing Pony'.

5 What great hound was permitted to speak only three times?

6 Sam's first child was named after what flower of Lothlórien?

7 How did King Théoden die?

8 Which Vala was known as the Giver of Fruits?

9 'An eye in a green face.' What?

10 In what likeness was the ship of Celeborn and Galadriel fashioned?

TIE BREAK

◆ What was the Sindarin name for the black crows of Fangorn and Dunland?

13 · THE ELVES

◆ How many Rings of Power had the Elves?

1 When the Elves awoke, what were the first things they beheld?

2 Which Vala did they revere above all others?

3 Name the three hosts of the Eldar which came to Aman.

4 Who married Melian the Maia?

5 Which Noldo created the Silmarils?

6 Why was the Doom of the Noldor wrought?

7 What was the last Kingdom of the Noldor to fall to Morgoth's legions?

8 Who were the Peredhil, what did the name mean, and what was unusual about their fate?

9 In the Second and Third Ages of the Sun, where did Círdan the Shipwright live?

10 What effect did the unmaking of the One Ring have on the remaining Elven realms of Middle-earth?

◆ Whose horse did Frodo ride across the Ford of Bruinen?

14 · FRODO BAGGINS

1 What was the name of Frodo's father?

2 What false name did Frodo adopt when he set out for Rivendell?

3 How did Frodo summon Tom Bombadil to the barrow-down?

4 Who took Frodo to be a long-lost cousin at 'The Prancing Pony'?

5 Who was Frodo delighted to find in the Hall of Fire?

6 How was Frodo protected from the Orc-spear in the Chamber of Mazarbul?

7 What was the last vision that Frodo saw in the Mirror of Galadriel?

8 What present did Galadriel give to Frodo?

9 How did Sam locate Frodo in the Tower of Cirith Ungol?

10 What anniversary from the War of the Ring troubled Frodo?

STARTER

◆ When Sting shone with a blue light, what did Bilbo know?

Match each weapon below with the character associated with it:

1 Glamdring	A. Bilbo
2 Andúril	B. Morgoth
3 Grond	C. Gandalf
4 Belthronding	D. Beleg
5 Sting	E. Théoden
6 Gurthang	F. Éomer
7 Herugrim	G. Aragorn
8 Gúthwinë	H. Túrin Turambar
9 Angrist	I. Gil-galad
10 Aeglos	J. Beren

TIE BREAK

◆ Who gave Túrin the name Mormegil (Black-sword)?

16 · GANDALF

♦ What was special about the diamond studs that Gandalf gave the Old Took?

1 What was Gandalf most famous for in the Shire?

2 Which of the three Elven-rings did Gandalf wield?

3 By what name was Gandalf known in his youth in Valinor?

4 What sword did Gandalf take from the Trolls' cave?

5 How did Gandalf finally confirm that Frodo's ring was indeed the One Ring?

6 How did Gandalf escape from the Tower of Orthanc?

7 What was the name of Gandalf's steed during the War of the Ring?

8 After the duel with the Balrog of Moria, how did Gandalf's appearance change?

9 Who did Gandalf lead to aid the defenders of Helm's Deep?

10 What were Gandalf's last words to Sam, Merry and Pippin at the Grey Havens?

TIE BREAK

♦ In TA 2063, where was Gandalf sent, and what was he unable to discover?

17 · ARCHITECTURE

STARTER

◆ How many corners did Bilbo's front door have?

1 What underground halls were known as the Thousand Caves?

2 What was most distinctive about the town of Esgaroth?

3 In what chamber did the Fellowship find Balin's tomb?

4 Where did Strider and the hobbits sleep in 'The Prancing Pony'?

5 What colour was the front door of Bag End?

6 What name did the Elves give to the wooden tree platforms in Lothlórien?

7 Who built the West-gate of Khazad-dûm?

8 What wall encircled the Pelennor Fields?

9 In what hall was there a carven image of a tree, inset with gems?

10 What and where were the Sammath Naur?

TIE BREAK

◆ What was the name of Manwë and Varda's halls on Taniquetil?

18 · FAMILY CONNECTIONS

STARTER

◆ Who was the son of Thráin II, King of the Dwarves?

Match the related characters and explain their family connection:

1	Théoden	A.	Amrod
2	Tuor	B.	Galdor
3	Aragorn	C.	Azog
4	Maedhros	D.	Eärendil
5	Thorin	E.	Arwen
6	Bolg	F.	Bilbo
7	Thingol	G.	Beregond
8	Túrin Turambar	H.	Éowyn
9	Sam Gamgee	I.	Melian
10	Bergil	J.	Fili

TIE BREAK

◆ Who were Nimloth of Doriath's mother- and father-in-law?

19 · J. R. R. Tolkien: A Biography – 1

- ◆ Was J. R. R. Tolkien a Doctor, a Professor or a Pastor?

1 Where and in what year was Ronald Tolkien born?

2 What step did Mabel Tolkien take in 1900, to the annoyance of her family?

3 In September 1900, Ronald gained entry into what school?

4 Tolkien based Hobbiton on which village outside Birmingham?

5 What was the T.C.B.S.?

6 After Tolkien's mother died, who became his legal guardian?

7 What did Tolkien initially study at Oxford?

8 What major character in *The Silmarillion* was inspired by a fragment of the *Crist* of Cynewulf?

9 What military skill did Tolkien specialise in during the Great War?

10 How did Tolkien come to write the opening line of *The Hobbit*?

Tie Break

- ◆ How did Tolkien fall in love with the Welsh language?

20 · Heights...

STARTER

◆ Who felt Sauron searching for him on the summit of Amon Hen?

1 On which mountain, and in which tower, were the halls of Manwë and Varda?

2 Why were the eagles obliged to Gandalf?

3 Who was hung by his right wrist from the face of Thangorodrim?

4 How high was the secret door in the side of the Lonely Mountain?

5 Who was cast over the Caragdûr in Gondolin, at Turgon's command?

6 Which members of the Fellowship fought to hold the walls of Helm's Deep?

7 Who gave the Carrock its name?

8 Upon which hill was the house of Mîm, the Petty-Dwarf?

9 What colour did Caradhras appear to be to the Fellowship?

10 Name three of the great Eagles of Arda.

TIE BREAK

◆ Why did Melkor raise the Misty Mountains?

21 ...AND DEPTHS

1 By what other name was the Lord of Waters known?

2 Who cast himself, and one of the Silmarils, into a chasm of fire?

3 What was the first great stronghold of Melkor?

4 Why did Beren prise only one Silmaril out of Morgoth's crown in Angband?

5 Who 'lived on a slimy island of rock' in the middle of a lake under the Misty Mountains?

6 Who was pinned by an Orc-spear in the Mines of Moria?

7 Who was the spouse of Ossë?

8 In the High-elven tongue, what were the Balrogs known as?

9 What gemstone did Bilbo pocket inside the Lonely Mountain?

10 Who dropped a stone into a well in the Mines of Moria?

22 · MISCELLANEOUS MIDDLE-EARTH – I

◆ Where was the Council of Elrond held?

1 Who had a butler called Galion?

2 What did Boromir advise the Fellowship to take with them to the Redhorn Gate?

3 What month was it when Frodo set out from Bag End for Rivendell?

4 Who or what were 'Yrch'?

5 Whose legs was Bilbo short enough to walk through?

6 Who seemed to know as much about the inside of Bilbo's larders as he did himself?

7 What did Sam cast into the air at the Three-Farthing Stone?

8 Whose purse could talk?

9 In the Hobbit poem 'Errantry', what were Dumbledors?

10 Who killed Saruman?

TIE BREAK

◆ Who for twenty-eight years saw only what Morgoth wanted him to see?

23 · WHO KILLED WHOM?

STARTER

◆ Who used the sunrise to kill trolls?

Match up the killers on the left with their victims on the right:

1 Beorn		A.	Finwë
2 Éowyn		B.	Glaurung
3 Melkor		C.	Smaug
4 Shagrat		D.	Bolg
5 Bard		E.	Azog
6 Túrin		F.	Aredhel
7 Fram		G.	Beren
8 Eöl		H.	Gorbag
9 Carcharoth		I.	The Nazgûl Lord
10 Dáin II		J.	Scatha

TIE BREAK

◆ Who was the intended victim of the dart that killed Aredhel?

24 · VALAQUENTA

◆ Which powerful beings did the Valar send to Middle-earth in c. TA 1000?

1 Who was the brother of Melkor in the thought of Ilúvatar?

2 In English, what title was he given?

3 What name did the Elves give to Varda?

4 Which Vala seldom clothed himself in a body?

5 Who was next in reverence to Varda among the Queens of the Valar, and who was her spouse?

6 Where did Námo live, and what was his role?

7 Where did Irmo and Estë live, and why did the Valar often come there?

8 From which Vala did Gandalf learn pity and endurance beyond hope?

9 Which Vala came last to Arda, and what did he delight in?

10 Who was called the Lord of Forests?

TIE BREAK

◆ Which Vala rarely came to the councils of the Valar?

25 · SAM GAMGEE

◆ What town did Sam hail from?

1 What was Sam by profession?

2 How did Gandalf come to select Sam to accompany Frodo to Rivendell?

3 Why did Sam particularly want to go to Rivendell?

4 What was 'as good a way of saying "here we are"' as he could think of, bar shouting?

5 Who or what did Sam have to leave behind at the Doors of Moria?

6 Where did he see a vision of Frodo lying asleep under a great dark cliff?

7 What happened when Sam tied the Elven rope around Gollum's ankle?

8 When did Sam realise that Frodo wasn't dead from the spider-venom?

9 Where did Sam plant the silver nut from Lothlórien, and what did it grow into?

10 How many times was he elected Mayor of the Shire?

TIE BREAK

◆ Why was Sam allowed to travel to the Undying Lands?

26 · ONE RING TO RULE THEM ALL

1 Who cut the One Ring from Sauron's hand?

2 How did the Ring betray him?

3 Why did Bilbo take so little hurt from the evil of the Ring?

4 Why did Bilbo have to let the dwarves into the secret of his ring?

5 After he returned to Bag End, what did Bilbo chiefly use the Ring for?

6 What happened when Frodo tried to cast the Ring into his fire?

7 What were the script and language of the fire-letters on the Ring?

8 Who didn't vanish when he put on the Ring?

9 Which member of the Fellowship demanded that Frodo give him the Ring?

10 At what moment did Sauron realise his great folly?

TIE BREAK

◆ At what battle did the Ring betray Isildur?

27 · WARRIORS

STARTER

♦ Who was so named because he once used an oak branch as a shield and weapon?

1 What type of Orcs acted as élite warriors and commanders in the War of the Ring?

2 What was Legolas's preferred weapon?

3 Who slew Uldor the Accursed?

4 Which warriors bore a white Elven S-rune on their helms?

5 Who was the Captain of the Rangers of Ithilien during the War of the Ring?

6 In which battle were Isildur and his three eldest sons slain?

7 What device did Gorbag's orcs bear on their shields?

8 Who were the Five Armies in the battle of the same name?

9 What was an *éored*?

10 What battle ended the Balchoth threat to Gondor?

TIE BREAK

♦ How was Muzgash the Orc killed?

28 · TOWNS AND CITIES

◆ What town lay over the hill from Overhill?

1 In what city was the Rath Dínen?

2 Who lived at Number 3 Bagshot Row, Hobbiton?

3 On what hill did the city of Tirion stand?

4 What and where was the Mathom-house?

5 How many levels was Minas Tirith built on?

6 In what Farthing was Michel Delving?

7 What does Minas Ithil mean in English?

8 In what city of Númenor was the court of the Kings?

9 What name was given to Fornost after it was abandoned?

10 Which city was the first capital of Gondor?

TIE BREAK

◆ What would probably have prevented Glaurung from destroying Nargothrond?

29· ODD MAN OUT - I

STARTER

◆ Who alone had to be blindfolded before entering Lórien?

In each of the following, which is the odd one out and why?

1 Bundashathûr, Barazinbar, Melian, The Lonely Mountain, Orodruin.

2 Smaug, Carcharoth, Brodda, Gothmog, Ungoliant.

3 Sam Gamgee, Boromir, Meriadoc Brandybuck, Legolas, Gollum.

4 Elostirion, Tol Galen, Orthanc, Annúminas, Minas Ithil.

5 Celegorm, Amrod, Amras, Maglor, Maeglin.

6 Sindar, Laiquendi, Vanyar, Nandor, Moriquendi.

7 caran, celeb, falas, mal, nim.

8 Uglúk, The Witch-King of Angmar, Shagrat, 'The Mouth of Sauron', Gorbag.

9 Narsil, Gurthang, Glamdring, Grond, Orcrist.

10 Dagorlad, The Field of Celebrant, The Pelennor Fields, Helm's Deep, The Tower Hills.

TIE BREAK

◆ Which one of these is an only child: Goldilocks Gamgee, Dior, Galadriel, Isildur, Faramir?

30 · GOLLUM

◆ Gollum's eyes were well-adapted to the sunlight. True or false?

1 What sort of creature was Gollum?

2 What was his original name?

3 Describe his physical appearance.

4 How many teeth did Gollum have?

5 What did he call the Ring?

6 How did he justify the way that he came by the Ring?

7 What did his diet mainly comprise in the Misty Mountains?

8 Who captured Gollum after Sauron released him?

9 Who reported to the Council of Elrond that Gollum had escaped from the Elves of Mirkwood?

10 What two names did Sam give him?

TIE BREAK

◆ What tasted like dust and ashes to Gollum?

31 · LEAF BY NIGGLE

1 What was the name of Niggle's neighbour?

2 Why did Niggle have to cycle into town?

3 What use did the Inspector of Houses want to make of his painting?

4 What were the two Voices discussing?

5 How did the doctor treat Niggle's sore hands?

6 What was labelled with Niggle's name?

7 Why did Niggle fall off his bicycle?

8 As time went on, where did Niggle turn his eyes more and more often?

9 Where did the last fragment of Niggle's painting end up?

10 When Niggle and Parish were told of the name of their country, what was their reaction?

TIE BREAK
◆ What essay, written at the same time as 'Leaf by Niggle', deals with similar themes?

STARTER

◆ Another name for goblin is (a) Balrog, (b) Sindar, (c) Crebain, (d) Orc, (e) Maia.

1 Mahtan was (a) a horse of the Rohirrim, (b) a Dwarf smith of Belegost, (c) the place of council of the Valar, (d) a Noldorin Elf, (e) the sword of Túrin Turambar.

2 Chuenya was (a) one of the Two Trees of Valinor, (b) a Quenya season, (c) a flower in Lothlórien, (d) a region of Gondor, (e) the Quenya name of Rivendell.

3 Narchost was (a) one of the Towers of the Teeth, (b) one of the great Dwarf mansions in Beleriand, (c) the greatest of the winged dragons, (d) one of the beacon-tower hills of Gondor, (e) the mighty sword of Elendil.

4 Celegorm was (a) the fifth King of Arthedain, (b) the son of Celeborn the Wise, (c) an Elvish name for Zirak-zigil, (d) the third son of Fëanor, (e) a stream in Brethil.

5 Oromë was (a) a lord of the Teleri, (b) one of the Maiar of Ulmo, (c) a Vala, (d) a hill in western Númenor, (e) the father of Gil-galad.

6 Flói was (a) one of Balin's companions in Khazad-dûm, (b) a Beorning, (c) the fourth King of Rohan, (d) the Queen of Durin the Deathless, (e) a woman of Gondor.

7 Arahael was (a) the name given to the eight chief Valar, (b) a herb, (c) a daughter of Elrond, (d) the capital city of Arnor, (e) a Chieftain of the Dúnedain of the North.

8 Dwaling was (a) a member of Thorin's Company, (b) a village in the Shire, (c) a fiefdom of Gondor, (d) a Ranger of Ithilien, (e) a month in the Shire calendar.

9 Nenya was (a) a pseudonym of Túrin, (b) a flower that grew on the funeral mounds of Edoras, (c) a *tengwa*, (d) the sister of Mandos and Lórien, (e) one of the Three Elven-rings.

10 Carc was (a) a Raven of Erebor, (b) a hobbit, (c) a star, (d) a Dwarf of Durin's Folk, (e) an Elda of the Vanyar.

TIE BREAK

◆ Minardil was (a) a Sindarin month, (b) a lord of Rohan, (c) a King of Gondor, (d) a sword, (e) an Elf of Doriath.

33 · THE DWARVISH VERSION

◆ Who, killing an Orc, said 'Now my count passes Master Legolas again'?

Match the Khuzdul names below with their Westron or Elvish equivalents:

1 Azanulbizar   A. Belegost

2 Khazad-dûm   B. Mirrormere

3 Gabilgathol   C. Naugrim

4 Kheled-zâram   D. Nogrod

5 Khazâd   E. Celebdil

6 Tumunzahar   F. The Dimrill Dale

7 Barazinbar   G. Fanuidhol

8 Bundushathûr   H. Caradhras

9 Nulukkizdîn   I. Nargothrond

10 Zirak-zigil   J. Moria

TIE BREAK

◆ Who told Túrin, 'You speak like a dwarf-lord of old; and at that I marvel'?

34 · ARAGORN

◆ Was Aragorn a Ranger, a Rider of Rohan, or a Raven?

1 By what name was Aragorn generally known in Bree?

2 Give both names for Aragorn's sword before and after it was re-forged.

3 What name was given to Aragorn when he served Ecthelion II?

4 Where was he raised?

5 When Frodo was wounded by the Nazgûl Lord, what did Aragorn go to fetch?

6 What compromise did Aragorn make when the Elves of Lórien insisted on blindfolding Gimli?

7 Who gave Aragorn Elessar, the Elfstone?

8 What name did Éomer give to Aragorn on account of his swift journey?

9 Who did Aragorn summon to the Stone of Erech?

10 Who crowned Aragorn King of Gondor, and who became his Queen?

TIE BREAK

◆ What did Elrond require of a man for him to marry Arwen?

35 · MISCELLANEOUS MIDDLE-EARTH – II

◆ Name the three volumes that *The Lord of the Rings* is commonly divided into.

1 What shape were the front door and windows of Bag End?

2 Who was famous in the Shire for his magical fireworks?

3 The town of Esgaroth stood on what lake?

4 Who rescued Thorin's Company from the wargs and the goblins of the Misty Mountains?

5 The 'Prancing Pony' inn was in what town?

6 How many Black Riders were there?

7 Where was the Last Homely House?

8 Who played a golden harp in Bilbo's house?

9 Where did Frodo have to take the One Ring to destroy it?

10 In what battle did King Théoden die?

TIE BREAK

◆ Who were generally the shortest: Elves, Dwarves or Hobbits?

36 · BEREN AND LÚTHIEN

STARTER

♦ Were Beren and Lúthien cousins, lovers or enemies?

1 Who were Lúthien's parents?

2 When Beren was forced to flee from Dorthonion, where did he resolve to go?

3 What name did he give to Lúthien and what does it mean in English?

4 Who betrayed Beren and Lúthien to Thingol?

5 What oath did Thingol swear to Lúthien concerning Beren?

6 Why did the Elves of Nargothrond not slay Beren?

7 Who helped Lúthien to escape from Nargothrond?

8 From whom did Beren take the knife Angrist?

9 How did Beren come by the name Erchamion?

10 What was unique about Lúthien's fate?

TIE BREAK

♦ What did Beren rescue at Rivil's Well above the Fen of Serech?

37 · MINOR CHARACTERS

◆ What was Barleyman Butterbur by profession?

1 Who asked Gandalf to lay aside his staff?

2 Who sold a pony to Butterbur for twelve silver pennies?

3 Where did Gaffer Gamgee send the Black Rider on to?

4 What was the relationship between Gollum and Déagol?

5 The Orc band that captured Merry and Pippin came from which three places?

6 Why did Frodo sometimes trespass on Farmer Maggot's land as a youngster?

7 Who was Haldir?

8 Morwen was the mother of which famous warrior?

9 Why did Bilbo leave Milo Burrows a gold pen and ink-bottle?

10 What name did Frodo suggest for Sam's first child?

TIE BREAK

◆ Where was Old Noakes of Bywater known to drink?

38 · CHAPTERS

◆ In which work would you find 'The Mirror of Galadriel?

Name the chapters that begin with the words below:

1 'Gandalf was gone, and the thudding hoofs of Shadowfax were lost in the night, when Merry came back to Aragorn.'

2 'When Bilbo opened his eyes, he wondered if he had; for it was just as dark as with them shut.'

3 'So it was that in the light of a fair morning King Théoden and Gandalf the White Rider met again upon the green grass beside the Deeping-stream.'

4 'The talk did not die down in nine or even ninety-nine days.'

5 'Of old there was Sauron the Maia, whom the Sindar in Beleriand named Gorthaur.'

6 'Bree was the chief village of the Bree-land, a small inhabited region, like an island in the empty lands round about.'

7 'Now if you wish, like the dwarves, to hear news of Smaug, you must go back again to the evening when he smashed the door and flew off in rage, two days before.'

8 'All about the hills the hosts of Mordor raged.'

9 'In that time were made those things that afterwards were most renowned of all the works of the Elves.'

10 'In a hole in the ground there lived a hobbit.'

TIE BREAK

◆ Which chapter *ends* with the following words: 'I am glad you are here with me. Here at the end of all things, Sam'?

39 · WHO AM I?

STARTER

◆ I have six teeth and remember sunlight on daisies. Who am I, my precious?

1 In which village was pipe-weed first cultivated?

2 Who was the mother of Fingolfin and Finarfin?

3 What was the Sindarin name for Weathertop?

4 What was the Shire's prison in Michel Delving called?

5 What river flowed past Menegroth before joining the Sirion?

6 Name the famous spear used by Gil-galad in the Battle of Dagorlad.

7 What name did Ghân-buri-Ghân give to the Orcs?

8 Who replaced Thorin as King under the Mountain?

9 Which Noldo invented the first writing system?

10 The initial letters of the answers to the questions above, when rearranged, spell out the name of a character. Name that character for a tenth point.

TIE BREAK

◆ I took Ulmo's message to Gondolin, and married Turgon's daughter, Idril. Who am I?

40 · ELVISH ELEMENTS

TARTER

◆ 'Elrond was an Elf.' How true is this?

Match the Elvish components below with their English equivalents:

1 Aina   A. Far and wide

2 Ang   B. Iron

3 Celeb   C. Shore

4 Dagor   D. Flower

5 Falas   E. Silver

6 Gond   F. Tower

7 Loth   G. Holy

8 Minas   H. Isle

9 Palan   I. Battle

10 Tol   J. Stone

TIE BREAK

◆ Alqualondë means 'Haven of......' what?

41 · THE WAR OF THE RING – I

◆ Which came first, the War of the Ring or the Quest of the Lonely Mountain?

1 How old was Frodo when Bilbo gave his farewell birthday party?

2 Who set out from Bag End with Frodo?

3 Name one of the Elves that the hobbits came across near Woodhall.

4 Who or what threatened to squeeze Merry in two?

5 What happened when Frodo fell off the table in 'The Prancing Pony'?

6 What did Frodo cry as he struck at the feet of the Nazgûl Lord?

7 Why were the Fellowship unable to pass through the Redhorn Gate?

8 What word opened the West-door of Moria?

9 What did Frodo fancy he saw in the darkness in Moria?

10 Which member of the Fellowship had to go blindfolded through Lothlórien?

TIE BREAK

◆ What lands did the Fellowship travel through just before reaching the Emyn Muil?

42 · GONDOR

1 What were the five great cities of Gondor at its height and what was its capital?

2 What disaster befell Gondor in 2002 TA?

3 What was the emblem of Elendil's heirs in Gondor?

4 How many walls encircled Minas Tirith?

5 Name three outlying regions whose representatives Pippin saw arriving to bolster Minas Tirith's strength.

6 Which member of the Fellowship swore an oath of allegiance to Denethor II?

7 What was the former name of Minas Tirith, and what did it mean?

8 Why did the name Boromir mean so much to the Rangers of Ithilien?

9 Who called Gondor Stoningland?

10 What did Denethor hold in his hands as he died on the funeral pyre?

43 · VITTLES

◆ What were the trolls sick of the taste of when Thorin's Company came across them?

1 Who taught his grandmother to suck eggs?

2 What was *lembas*?

3 Who lived mostly on cream and honey?

4 Whose beer was laid under an enchantment of surpassing excellence for seven years?

5 What crop was Farmer Maggot famous for?

6 Why did Pippin want to visit the 'Golden Perch' at Stock?

7 Why did Merry and Pippin become the tallest hobbits in recorded Shire history?

8 'Never thirsty, ever drinking,
All in mail never clinking.' What?

9 Who said he could eat anything in the wide world right then for hours on end – but not an apple?

10 Who hungered for and devoured light?

TIE BREAK
◆ Who asked Bilbo for pork-pie and salad?

44 · MERRY

STARTER

◆ Did Merry come from Hobbiton or Buckland?

1 What was Merry's real name in genuine Hobbitish?

2 Who found him lying by the roadside in Bree?

3 Who treated a wound on Merry's forehead?

4 What was Merry doing when Théoden's company found him in Isengard?

5 Whose esquire did he become?

6 Who or what was Stybba?

7 How did Merry save Éowyn's life?

8 What did Éomer and Éowyn give to Merry as a farewell present?

9 Who did he marry?

10 Name two scholarly works that Merry wrote.

TIE BREAK

◆ How did Merry grow three inches during the War of the Ring?

45 · ORCS

◆ Where did Thorin's Company first meet Orcs (goblins)?

1 How did Melkor breed the race of Orcs?

2 What colour was their skin?

3 Where did Orcs and Elves fight the first battle of the Wars of Beleriand?

4 In what battle did Glaurung lead the Orcs to victory over the Noldor, breaking the Siege of Angband?

5 What name was given to the greater Orcs who had no fear of sunlight?

6 What was the capital of the Orcs of the Misty Montains?

7 Who was the Orc chieftain at the Battle of Azanulbizar?

8 During the Quest of the Lonely Mountain, who killed the Great Goblin?

9 Where did Gorbag's Orcs come from?

10 Who were the *snaga*, and what did the name mean?

TIE BREAK

◆ The Orc who speared Frodo in Khazad-dûm was slain with which sword?

STARTER

♦ What kind of being was Saruman?

1 What did the Elves call Saruman, and what did it mean?

2 In what field was he especially knowledgeable?

3 Why did he wish the Necromancer to remain in Dol Guldur?

4 How did Sauron ensnare Saruman?

5 What device did Saruman's Orcs bear on their helms?

6 Which member of the Court of Rohan secretly served Saruman?

7 Saruman exchanged white garments for what?

8 What was the likely origin of Saruman's nickname 'Sharkey'?

9 Who unwittingly sent Gandalf to imprisonment in Orthanc?

10 What happened to Saruman after Gríma killed him?

TIE BREAK

♦ 'Saruman, you missed your path in life', said Gandalf. What career should Saruman have chosen?

47 · WHO SANG THAT?

STARTER

◆ Who teased Bilbo with a song about his crockery?

Name the singers of these songs:

1 In western lands beneath the Sun
    the flowers may rise in Spring,
the trees may bud, the waters run,
    the merry finches sing.

2 Farewell sweet earth and northern sky,
for ever blest, since here did lie
and here with lissom limbs did run
beneath the Moon, beneath the Sun,
Lúthien Tinúviel
more fair than mortal tongue can tell.

3 Far over the misty mountains cold
To dungeons deep and caverns old
We must away ere break of day,
To seek the pale enchanted gold.

4 There is an inn, a merry old inn
    beneath an old grey hill,
And there they brew a beer so brown
That the Man in the Moon himself came down
    one night to drink his fill.

5 Old fat spider spinning in a tree!
Old fat spider can't see me!

6 To the Sea, to the Sea! The white gulls are crying,
The wind is blowing, and the white foam is flying.

7 Cold be hand and heart and bone,
And cold be sleep under stone:
never more to wake on stony bed,
never, till the Sun fails and the Moon is dead.

8 Troll sat alone on his seat of stone,
And munched and mumbled a bare old bone.

9 The dragon is withered,
His bones are now crumbled;
His armour is shivered,
His splendour is humbled!

10 When Spring unfolds the beechen leaf, and sap is in the
bough;
When light is on the wild-wood stream, and wind is on the
brow;
When stride is long, and breath is deep, and keen the
mountain-air,
Come back to me! Come back to me, and say my land is
fair!

TIE BREAK

◆ Who 'chanted a song of wizardry, of piercing, opening, of
treachery'?

48 · J. R. R. Tolkien: A Chronology

Starter

◆ Tolkien was born in which century?

Match each date with its corresponding event:

1 21 September 1937   A. Ronald and Edith are married.

2 14 November 1904   B. Tolkien becomes Merton Professor of English Language and Literature.

3 August 1954   C. Publication of *The Fellowship of The Ring*.

4 Spring 1972   D. Mabel Tolkien dies of diabetes.

5 22 March 1916   E. Birth of eldest son, John.

6 29 November 1971   F. Tolkien receives the CBE.

7 June 1965   G. Publication of *The Hobbit*.

8 16 November 1917   H. Mabel Tolkien received into the Catholic Church.

9 Autumn 1945   I. Edith Tolkien dies.

10 June 1900   J. Ace Books publish an unauthorised edition of *The Lord of the Rings*.

Tie Break

◆ In autumn 1920, Tolkien began work at which University?

49 · TOWERS

STARTER

◆ In what land was Barad-dûr, the Dark Tower?

1 In which tower was the Master-stone of the palantíri kept?

2 What tower was guarded by the Two Watchers?

3 What was the Tower of Orthanc made of?

4 By what respective names were Minas Tirith and Minas Morgul formerly known?

5 Name and Towers of the Teeth.

6 What was the tallest of the White Towers?

7 Who built Barad Nimras and where?

8 Why could Barad-dûr not be destroyed entirely at the end of the Second Age?

9 What colour was the great Tower of Minas Tirith?

10 What tower guarded Hithlum from assault from Angband?

TIE BREAK

◆ The artificial trees Glingal and Bethil stood in the Tower of the King in which city?

STARTER

◆ In what island did Farmer Giles live?

1 What was Farmer Giles' full name?

2 What was his dog called?

3 What did Giles stuff into his blunderbuss?

4 What did the giant think had happened when Giles shot at him?

5 What two things did the King send Giles on the feast of St Michael?

6 At the King's Christmas Feast, what was served in place of Dragon's Tail?

7 What was the name of the dragon that landed in the realm of Augustus Bonifacius?

8 What was Tailbiter's Latin name?

9 Who advised Giles to take some stout rope with him?

10 What new order of knighthood was created under King Ægidius?

TIE BREAK

◆ What was Sam the smith's predominant mood?

51 · WHO SAID...? – II

◆ Who trusted that Bilbo would be *punctual*?

Who said the following:

1 'I don't need your service, thank you, but I expect you need mine.'

2 'Why, I feel all thin, sort of *stretched*, if you know what I mean: like butter that has been scraped over too much bread.'

3 'If any mortals have claim to the Ring, it is the men of Númenor, and not Halflings.'

4 'Go on! Go on! I will do the stinging!'

5 'Yes, I am white now. Indeed I *am* Saruman, one might almost say, Saruman as he should have been.'

6 'Lovely titles! But lucky numbers don't always come off.'

7 'It is not as I would have it; for this is little like my fair house in Edoras.'

8 'Death! Ride, ride to ruin and the world's ending!'

9 'My poor legs, my poor legs!'

10 'Baruk Khazâd! Khazâd ai-mênu!'

TIE BREAK

◆ Who told Frodo that '.........what concerns Boromir concerns me'?

STARTER

◆ Thorin's Company passed through Mirkwood in which chapter of *The Hobbit*: 'Riddles in the Dark', 'Flies and Spiders' or 'Inside Information'?

1 In what region did Mirkwood lie, and what did it mean in English?

2 By what name was Mirkwood formerly known?

3 What was the name of Sauron's stronghold in Southern Mirkwood?

4 Name a king of the Elves of Mirkwood.

5 Why did Beorn warn Thorin's Company against drinking from the stream in Mirkwood?

6 In the darkness, what sort of eyes did Bilbo least like the look of, and what guess did he venture as to their owners?

7 Which dwarf fell under the spell of the enchanted stream in Mirkwood?

8 What colour were the butterflies that Bilbo saw above the roof of the forest?

9 After killing a giant spider, what name did Bilbo give to his sword?

10 What was the Elvenking wearing on his head when Bilbo first saw him?

TIE BREAK

◆ What happened to Mirkwood after the War of the Ring?

53 · SHIPS AND SEAFARERS

◆ The Grey Havens lay due North, East or West from the Shire?

1 Which host of the Eldar were called the Falmari, and what did it mean?

2 How did the Vanyar and Noldor cross from Beleriand into Aman?

3 Who taught the Teleri the art of ship-building?

4 What kind of birds drew the ships of the Teleri to the shores of Aman?

5 Who helped build Vingilot for Eärendil?

6 What does Alqualondë mean in English?

7 What were the two chief ports of the Falas?

8 Whose ship was called Alcarondas?

9 The Elendili escaped the Downfall of Númenor in how many ships?

10 Who defeated the Umbar fleet in the War of the Ring?

TIE BREAK

◆ The Ship-kings of the Third Age expanded which Kingdom with their fleets?

◆ What job description did Thorin and Gandalf give Bilbo: Burglar, Scout or Assassin?

1 Who, or what, was Niphredil?

2 How did Snaga of Cirith Ungol die?

3 Orcs are to Uruk-hai as Trolls are to what?

4 What made Sam so certain that Frodo had been killed by Shelob?

5 Who 'munched and mumbled a bare old bone'?

6 Who was the Dark Elf of Nan Elmoth?

7 Beside which lake did the Elves awake?

8 Whose handmaid was Ilmarë?

9 What did Gandalf implore Thorin's Company not to do in Mirkwood?

10 What region was added to the Shire by gift of Elessar?

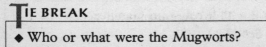

TIE BREAK

◆ Who or what were the Mugworts?

55 · TOLKIEN FANDOM

STARTER

◆ In which country did Tolkien's popularity most explode in the Sixties?

1 Tolkien received a letter from a namesake of which major character in *The Lord of the Rings*?

2 Messrs. Ackerman, Zimmerman and Brodax approached Tolkien with what proposal?

3 What happened in 1965 to dramatically boost sales of *The Hobbit* and *The Lord of the Rings*?

4 What was in the cover picture on Ballantine's 1965 American edition of *The Hobbit*?

5 The Mythopoeic Society was devoted to studying the works of which three authors?

6 Who founded the Tolkien Society of America?

7 The Ring Road around which university campus was renamed by the students 'Tolkien Road'?

8 What was *Gandalf's Garden*?

9 Who published a book about Tolkien which he found 'insulting and offensive'?

10 What game, largely inspired by Tolkien, did Gary Gygax create in the mid-Seventies?

TIE BREAK

◆ After corresponding with a real Sam Gamgee, who did Tolkien fear receiving a letter from?

STARTER

◆ Was Pippin a member of the Fellowship of the Ring?

1 What was Pippin's full name?

2 Who was his father?

3 How did Gandalf react when Pippin dropped a stone down a well in Moria?

4 What did Pippin drop as a sign to any pursuers while he was a prisoner of the Orc-band?

5 Who took Merry and Pippin to his house during the Entmoot?

6 How did Pippin come to be questioned by Sauron?

7 Who did Pippin swear fealty and service to?

8 What was the name of Pippin's only child?

9 Elessar appointed Pippin to what office?

10 Where were Merry and Pippin laid to rest?

TIE BREAK

◆ 'And how light his footfalls are!' Who or what was Pippin talking about?

57 · KHAZAD-DÛM

STARTER

◆ The Orcs of the Misty Mountains delved Khazad-dûm.
True or false?

1 What name was given to Khazad-dûm in the Westron?

2 What valley lay outside the Great Gates of Khazad-dûm?

3 What did the Dwarves accidentally release while tunnelling in TA 1980?

4 Which member of Thorin's Company led an expedition to re-colonise Khazad-dûm?

5 Which peak did the Endless Stair lead up to?

6 What precious metal was discovered in Khazad-dûm early in the Second Age?

7 Why was the Sirannon only a trickle when the Fellowship came to Khazad-dûm?

8 Why did Gandalf have difficulty in opening the West-door?

9 Whose emblem was the single star on the West-door?

10 What were the last words written by Ori in the record of Balin's people?

TIE BREAK

◆ How many toes had the foot which Frodo stabbed at the door of Mazarbul?

58 · DRAGONS

◆ Which Dragon smelt Bilbo and felt his air?

1 Name the three varieties of Dragon.

2 What colour was Dragon-blood?

3 Who was named the Father of Dragons?

4 Why was Morgoth displeased with him?

5 In the Fifth Battle of Beleriand, who were the only Allies who could withstand the Dragon-flame?

6 With what sword did Túrin Turambar slay Glaurung?

7 In the War of Wrath, who contended with the Dragons in the air?

8 What was the name of the Dragon that Fram son of Frumgar slew?

9 Which Dragon destroyed Dale and took The Lonely Mountain for his own?

10 Who slew Smaug?

TIE BREAK

◆ Which battle revealed the full power of Glaurung to the Elves?

59 · IN VALINOR

◆ Was the land of Valinor home to the Valar, the Sindar or the Dwarves?

1 What was the Quenya name for the Ring of Doom, where the Valar held council?

2 Name the Two Trees of Valinor.

3 What mountains lay on the Eastern coast of Valinor?

4 Upon what mound did the Two Trees of Valinor stand?

5 What was the only city in Valinor?

6 After the Darkening of Valinor, where did the light of the Two Trees live on?

7 What oath did Fëanor and his sons swear on the summit of Túna?

8 What became of the single fruits that Telperion and Laurelin bore before they died?

9 Who ruled the remnant of the Noldor that stayed in Valinor?

10 What string of islands prevented all but one mariner from sailing from Middle-earth to the Undying Lands?

TIE BREAK

◆ When Melkor departed southwards from Valinor, which Valar searched for him to the North, expecting him to return to his old strongholds in northern Middle-earth?

STARTER

◆ Describe the first Nazgûl that Frodo saw.

1 In what language did 'Nazgûl' mean 'Ringwraith'?

2 How many Nazgûl were there, and what were they originally?

3 How did Sauron ensnare the Nine?

4 What Northern Kingdom in the Third Age was ruled by the Lord of the Nazgûl?

5 When in Dol Guldur, why did Sauron send the other eight to Mordor?

6 When Minas Ithil fell to the Ringwraiths, what new name was it given, and what did it mean?

7 How many Black Riders did Frodo espy from the summit of Weathertop?

8 What was most dangerous about the wound inflicted on Frodo by the Nazgûl Lord?

9 What happened to the Black Riders at the Ford of Rivendell?

10 Who slew the Lord of the Nazgûl?

TIE BREAK

◆ Who fled from the Nazgûl at the house at Crickhollow?

◆ List any four Hobbits.

List the following:

1 All of the Nine Walkers.

2 Any seven of Sam Gamgee's children.

3 The seven sons of Fëanor.

4 The Elvish names of the three great peaks above Moria.

5 All five mortal bearers of the One Ring.

6 All fifteen participants in the Quest of the Lonely Mountain.

7 The eight Aratar.

8 The Elvish names of the three Dwarf-mansions mentioned in the Elven histories.

9 The three Elven Rings.

10 The three Trolls found by Bilbo and his companions.

TIE BREAK

◆ List any four races of Northmen.

62 · RIVENDELL

STARTER

◆ Who rested at Rivendell on their way to the Lonely Mountain?

1 What road led from Bree to Rivendell?

2 What was Rivendell called in Sindarin?

3 Who founded Rivendell?

4 Rivendell was sustained by the power of what ring?

5 What did Elrond discover about the map of the Lonely Mountain?

6 The Ford of Rivendell crossed which river?

7 Who was Elrond's daughter?

8 Why did Boromir travel from Gondor to Rivendell?

9 Who was the first to utter the Black Speech in Rivendell?

10 What news did Legolas bring to the Council of Elrond?

TIE BREAK

◆ As Gandalf reported to the Council of Elrond, what fate had Saruman claimed for the One Ring?

63 · ROADS AND RIVERS

STARTER

◆ What were Gandalf's last words to Bilbo and the Dwarves before they entered Mirkwood?

1 Of which river was the Adurant a tributary?

2 What road crossed the River Poros?

3 What city stood at the meeting of the Glanduin and Mitheithel?

4 Tol-in-Gaurhoth stood on what river?

5 What was the Greenway formerly known as?

6 Déagol found the One Ring in which river?

7 The Falls of Sirion plunged over which range of hills?

8 What river was called Kibil-nâla in the Khuzdul?

9 The River Running flowed into what body of water?

10 Where did the Great East Road end in the West?

TIE BREAK

◆ What stood in the Anduin West of Beorn's house?

STARTER

◆ Which of the following is an Elvish word: Lithlad, Nulukkizdîn, Éowyn?

Match the Elvish words and names below with their English equivalents:

1 Lúva   A. Mighty

2 Elrond   B. Letters

3 Laurelin   C. Bow

4 Tengwar   D. Hill of Sorcery

5 Beleg   E. Land of Pines

6 Dol Guldur   F. Star-dome

7 Taniquetil   G. Tower of Sorcery

8 Minas Morgul   H. Spirit of Fire

9 Dorthonion   I. Song of Gold

10 Fëanor   J. High White Peak

TIE BREAK

◆ Ondolindë was the original name of which city?

65 · WEAPONS

STARTER

◆ Was Bilbo's knife, Sting, forged by the Dwarves?

1 With what weapon did Eöl slay Aredhel?

2 What name was given to Glamdring by the Orcs?

3 What name was given to Anglachel when it was re-forged?

4 Who forged the blades that the hobbits took from the Barrow-mound?

5 What kind of weapon did the Lord of the Nazgûl wield in the Battle of the Pelennor Fields?

6 Whose bow was called Belthronding?

7 Who forged Narsil and Angrist?

8 What weapons did the Balrog of Khazad-dûm wield when it faced Gandalf?

9 Why was there a notch in Gimli's axe after the Battle of the Hornburg?

10 How was Gríma Wormtongue killed?

TIE BREAK

◆ How were the Teleri mainly armed at the Kinslaying?

Starter

◆ Who is described here? 'There he lay, a vast red-golden dragon, fast asleep; a thrumming came from his jaws and nostrils, and wisps of smoke, but his fires were low in slumber.'

Identify the characters described below:

1 'He had a tall pointed blue hat, a long grey cloak, a silver scarf over which his long white beard hung down below his waist, and immense black boots.'

2 'A man so bent with age that he seemed almost a dwarf; but his white hair was long and thick and fell in great braids from beneath a thin golden circlet set upon his brow.'

3 'Standing near was a huge man with a thick black beard and hair, and great bare arms and legs with knotted muscles. He was clothed in a tunic of wool down to his knees, and was leaning on a large axe.'

4 'A strange-looking weather-beaten man, sitting in the shadows near the wall, was also listening intently to the hobbit-talk. He had a tall tankard in front of him, and was smoking a long-stemmed pipe curiously carved.'

5 'Blue was her raiment as the unclouded heaven, but her eyes were grey as the starlit evening; her mantle was sewn with golden flowers, but her hair was dark as the shadows of twilight.'

6 'He was too large and heavy for a hobbit, if not quite tall enough for one of the Big People, though he made noise enough for one, stumping along with great yellow boots on his thick legs.'

7 'A large Man-like, almost Troll-like, figure, at least fourteen foot high, very sturdy, with a tall head, and hardly any neck.'

8 'Their captain was ...., grim-voiced and grim-faced, whose friends had accused him of prophesying floods and poisoned fish, though they knew his worth and courage.'

9 'His beard, very long and forked, was white, nearly as white as the snow-white cloth of his garments. He wore a silver belt, and round his neck hung a chain of silver and diamonds.'

10 'The face of .... was ageless, neither old nor young, though in it was written the memory of many things both glad and sorrowful.'

TIE BREAK

◆ Who is this? 'For the arising of .... was terrible, as a mounting wave that strides to the land, with dark helm foam-crested and raiment of mail shimmering from silver down into shadows of green.'

STARTER

◆ *The Lord of the Rings*/is one of those things:/if you like it, you do:/if you don't, then ………' what?

1 Who wrote to his father, saying that *The Hobbit* was 'good and should appeal to all children between the ages of 5 and 9'?

2 In which two journals did C. S. Lewis enthuse about *The Hobbit* shortly after its publication?

3 Which three notable writers contributed to the 'blurb' inside the dustjacket of the first edition of *The Fellowship of the Ring*?

4 Who was apprehensive that he could 'find no really adequate reasons' for taking *The Fellowship of the Ring* seriously?

5 What publication dismissed the first volume as 'so many pages of small talk and muddle'?

6 What poet concluded of *The Fellowship of the Ring* that 'No fiction I have read in the last five years has given me more joy'?

7 What kind of reception did the American magazine *New Republic* give to *The Lord of the Rings*?

8 What was the main criticism in Edwin Muir's review of *The Lord of the Rings*, entitled 'A Boy's World'?

9 Who was comforted 'to be once more assured that the meek shall inherit the earth'?

10 What was Tolkien's attitude to the aggressive polarity of opinions over *The Lord of the Rings*?

TIE BREAK

◆ Which newspaper said, 'He has the air of inventing nothing. He has studied trolls and dragons at first hand and describes them with fidelity'?

68 · MEN

1 Why did Elves call Men the Engwar?

2 Who was the only man to come back from the mansions of the dead?

3 Who first discovered Men in Beleriand?

4 Why did the Green-elves of Ossiriand object to the presence of Men in their land?

5 Name the three Houses of the Edain.

6 What two Kingdoms did the Elendili establish in Middle-earth after the Downfall of Númenor?

7 What name was given to the survivors of the destruction of Arnor?

8 What disaster befell Gondor in TA 1636–7?

9 Who killed the Orc chieftain Bolg at the Battle of Five Armies?

10 What race of Men populated Umbar?

69 · Missing Links

◆ Fill in the gap in the start of the Dwarf song:

Far over the misty mountains cold
To dungeons deep and .... old

Fill in the gaps in the following songs or poems:

1 In .... beneath the Sun,
   the flowers may rise in Spring

2 There .... fell, ... mighty,
   to his golden halls and green pastures
   in the Northern fields never returning,
   high lord of the host.

3 .... am I, Biggest of all, Huge, old, and tall.

4 Fifteen .... in five ....,
   their feathers were fanned in a fiery breeze!

5 Learn now the lore of ....!
   First name the four, the ....

6 From dark .... in the dim morning
   with thane and captain rode Thengel's son

7 .... was an Elven-king.
   Of him the harpers sadly sing

8 Faithful servant yet master's bane, Lightfoot's foal,
   swift ....

9 .... was a mariner that tarried in ....

10 Old ...., all big body, Old .... can't spy me!

Tie Break

◆ Complete the following, from the West-door of Khazad-dûm: 'Ennyn Durin Aran Moria: pedo .... a minno'.

◆ Which book deals with the Wars in detail: *The Hobbit*, *The Lord of the Rings* or *The Silmarillion*?

---

1 How many major battles were there during the Wars of Beleriand?

2 Who led the Elves of Ossiriand to Thingol's aid in the first major battle of the Wars?

3 What happened to the Orcs that survived the First Battle?

4 What name was given to the Second Battle, and where was it fought?

5 What fatal mistake did Fëanor make after the Second Battle?

6 Which great servant of Morgoth issued forth from Angband two hundred years after Dagor Aglareb?

7 The Siege of Angband ended with what battle?

8 What name was given to the land of Ard-galen after its desolation by Morgoth, and what did it mean in English?

9 What role did the sons of Ulfang play in the Nirnaeth Arnoediad?

10 What was Morgoth's final gambit in the War of Wrath?

TIE BREAK

◆ Who gave Morgoth seven wounds in a duel?

STARTER

◆ Who was son of Primula Brandybuck and great-grandson of the Old Took?

1 Who was the father of Uldor, Ulfast and Ulwarth?

2 Which of Sam's daughters married Pippin's son, Faramir?

3 How were Galadriel and Finrod Felagund related?

4 Who did Finwë marry after the death of Míriel?

5 How much Maia blood was there in Dior?

6 Where did Pippin's wife come from?

7 What was the real name of Sam's father?

8 How many brothers and sisters did Bilbo have?

9 Name Thorin Oakenshield's father and grandfather respectively.

10 How were Boromir and Finduilas related?

TIE BREAK

◆ Why would Gimli have had a genealogical reason to hate the Watcher in the Water?

STARTER

◆ Who made a sign on Bilbo's door, saying 'Burglar wants a good job, plenty of Excitement and reasonable Reward'?

Match the emblems below with the people or places that they represent:

1 A white hand on a black field   A. Durin's Folk

2 An anvil and hammer surmounted by a crown with seven stars   B. Sauron

3 A moon disfigured by a death's head   C. Rohan

4 A white tree under seven stars and a silver crown, on a black field   D. The House of Fëanor

5 A white horse on a green field   E. The House of Fingolfin

6 A red lidless eye   F. Saruman

7 A winged sun   G. Dol Amroth

8 Blue and silver   H. Minas Morgul

9 An eight-rayed silver star   I. Elendil

10 A white swan-ship on a blue field   J. Finwë

TIE BREAK

◆ In the Battle of Unnumbered Tears, whose banners did the Elves of Nargothrond raise before the walls of Angband?

STARTER

◆ List *The Silmarillion*, *The Hobbit* and *The Lord of the Rings* in the order in which they were published.hoierjgh

1 Why was Susan Dagnall important to Tolkien's career?

2 Who gave *The Hobbit* a glowing review in *The Times* shortly after its publication?

3 What name did Tolkien originally give to the character of Frodo Baggins?

4 What did Tolkien 'cordially dislike in all its manifestations'?

5 What short story hinted at Tolkien's fear of not being able to complete his mythology?

6 Why did Tolkien send regular correspondence to South Africa during 1944?

7 Why was Tolkien keen to let Collins, not Allen & Unwin, publish *The Lord of the Rings*?

8 Why was *The Return of the King* only published after some delay?

9 Who wrote in *Truth* that he believed *The Lord of the Rings* to be 'one of the most remarkable works of literature in our, or any, time'?

10 The gravestone of Ronald and Edith Tolkien bears the names of which characters from Middle-earth?

TIE BREAK

◆ What was the T. C. B. S.?

74 · LEGOLAS

◆ What was Legolas's favoured weapon?

1 Who was Legolas's father?

2 What does 'Legolas' mean in English?

3 What colours did Legolas usually wear?

4 What gifts did he receive from Galadriel?

5 Who or what did Legolas shoot out of the sky from the bank of the Anduin?

6 Name the horse that Éomer lent to Legolas and Gimli.

7 Where did Legolas feel the air throbbing in his ears?

8 Where did Legolas promise to go with Gimli after the War of the Ring was over?

9 What land did he help restore to its former beauty after the War of the Ring?

10 When Legolas sailed West over the Sea, which other member of the Fellowship reportedly went with him?

TIE BREAK

◆ Where did Legolas see the Sea for the first time?

75 · CHARACTERS

◆ 'I am the friend of bears and the guest of eagles. I am Ringwinner and Luckwearer; and I am Barrel-rider.' Who am I?

Pair up the names that refer to the same character:

1 Tinúviel		**A.** Fëanor
2 Eärendil		**B.** Incánus
3 Araw		**C.** Eru
4 Curufinwë		**D.** Gil-Estel
5 Strider		**E.** Aragorn
6 Tom Bombadil		**F.** Gil-galad
7 Tharkûn		**G.** Oromë
8 Éowyn		**H.** Iarwain Ben-adar
9 Ilúvatar		**I.** Lúthien
10 Ereinion		**J.** Dernhelm

TIE BREAK

◆ Which tragic figure was known as Thalion, the Steadfast?

76 · THE ISTARI

STARTER

◆ What were the Istari? (a) constellations, (b) swords, (c) Dwarf-lords, (d) Wizards, (e) flowers of Gondor.

1 How many Istari were there?

2 What sort of beings were they, and what form did they take?

3 In what Age did they arrive at the Grey Havens?

4 Who were the three named Istari?

5 Who was counted the greatest of the Istari in the Fourth Age?

6 What colour was associated with Radagast?

7 Where did Radagast live?

8 Who granted Saruman the key to the tower of Orthanc?

9 What act completed Gandalf's task upon Middle-earth?

10 Who slew Saruman?

TIE BREAK

◆ Name three members of the White Council other than Gandalf and Saruman.

77 · BATTLES

◆ Who made the least obvious target at the Battle of Five Armies, and why?

1 Who won fame by killing Azog in the Battle of Azanulbizar?

2 In what battle did Merry and Pippin lead a band of hobbits against a hundred or so of the Chief's Men?

3 At the Battle of Greenfields, who was said to have invented the game of golf, and how?

4 Who defeated whom in the Battle of the Camp?

5 Durin's Tower and the top of Endless Stair were destroyed in what battle?

6 Who led the army of Nargothrond in the Battle of Tumhalad?

7 Who replaced the Lord of the Nazgûl as commander of Sauron's forces in the Battle of the Pelennor Fields?

8 At what battle was the army of the Witch-king annihilated?

9 In the Battle of the Field of Celebrant, who led the Éothéod to the aid of the Northern Army?

10 What battle was fought on and around Erebor in TA 2941?

TIE BREAK

◆ What was Morgoth's last desperate gambit in the Great Battle, the War of Wrath?

78 · GONDOLIN

◆ Why wasn't the view of the city of Gondolin familiar across all the land?

1 Who built Gondolin and where?

2 What city was it modelled on?

3 Why did Ulmo command Turgon to leave arms and a sword in his house in Nevrast?

4 What were Belthil and Glingal?

5 What was the Sindarin name for the Encircling Mountains?

6 By what other name was Eöl known, and who did he take to wife?

7 Over what precipice was Eöl cast?

8 Who cried out to Turgon in Dimbar, and what did this tell Morgoth?

9 Why did Maeglin hate Tuor so much?

10 Who slew Gothmog in defence of Gondolin?

TIE BREAK

◆ How did Glorfindel die?

STARTER

◆ 'The dark fire will not avail you, flame of Udûn. Go back to the Shadow! You cannot pass.' Who was Gandalf talking to?

1 Whom did Sam succeed as Mayor of the Shire?

2 On what day of what year was the Battle of the Pelennor Fields fought?

3 Who was Merry's mother?

4 What was the Sindarin name for the Tree of Tirion?

5 What number was Ar-Pharazôn in the line of the Kings of Númenor?

6 Who forged Anglachel and Anguirel?

7 What name was given to the Eldar who were 'not of Aman'?

8 How did Óin die?

9 What was Ithildin?

10 What was Overlithe?

TIE BREAK

◆ 'But our need is for aid in battle,' said Éomer. 'How will you and your folk help us?' Who was Éomer talking to?

STARTER

◆ What day in the Dwarves' year was Durin's Day?

Pair up each date with its corresponding event:

1 3441 SA   **A.** Death of Elros Tar-Minyatur

2 1409 TA   **B.** Sauron taken as prisoner to Númenor

3 2994 TA   **C.** The Fell Winter. White Wolves invade Eriador from the North

4 2790 TA   **D.** The Witch-king of Angmar invades Arnor

5 3 October 3018 TA   **E** Sauron overthrown by Elendil and Gil-galad

6 15 January 3019 TA   **F.** The Council of Elrond

7 442 SA   **G.** Balin perishes in Moria

8 2911 TA   **H.** Gandalf attacked at night on Weathertop

9 3262 SA   **I.** Gandalf confronts the Balrog of Khazad-dûm

10 25 October 3018 TA   **J.** Thrór slain by an Orc in Moria

TIE BREAK

◆ In what year of the Third Age did Isildur plant a seedling of the White Tree in Minas Anor?

81 · MORDOR

STARTER

◆ Who told Frodo, 'Alas! Mordor draws all wicked things, and the Dark Power was bending all its will to gather them there'?

1 What does 'Mordor' mean in English?

2 What mountains bounded Mordor to the north?

3 Name the plain that lay between Isenmouthe and Cirith Gorgor.

4 Who built Durthang and why?

5 What pass was guarded by the Towers of the Teeth?

6 What was Barad-dûr called in Orkish?

7 What was most distinctive about the flies of Mordor?

8 Shelob's Lair was called what in Sindarin?

9 How did Frodo and Sam escape from the Orc-band marching to Udûn?

10 What was Gollum's last wail as he fell into the abyss?

TIE BREAK

◆ The tracker Orc told the Uruk to 'Go to your filthy Shriekers, and may they freeze the flesh off you!' Who were the 'Shriekers'?

STARTER

◆ Roughly how long did Bilbo's journey to the Lonely Mountain and back take?

1 Who set out for Rivendell on his eleventy-first birthday?

2 Which members of the Fellowship trod the Paths of the Dead?

3 How did Fingolfin and his people return to Middle-earth from Valinor?

4 What name was given to the Elves who refused the Great Journey, and what did it mean in English?

5 Who journeyed to Morgoth's throne disguised as a great wolf and a vampire-bat?

6 At whose bidding did Tuor seek out Gondolin?

7 What time of day was it when Bilbo set out to join Thorin's Company?

8 What food did the Men of Esgaroth make for long journeys?

9 Who did Merry ride with when the Rohirrim set out to aid Minas Tirith?

10 Name five of the company that sailed with Frodo from the Grey Havens.

TIE BREAK

◆ By seizing all the ships on the flight from Valinor, what fate did Fëanor leave for Fingolfin's people?

83 · ODD MAN OUT - II

STARTER

◆ Which of the following was not a member of the Fellowship of the Ring: Pippin, Gimli, Boromir, Arathorn, Sam?

In each of the following, which is the odd man out, and why?

1 Ossë, Manwë, Ilmarë, Olórin, Eonwë.

2 Mîm, Glóin, Telchar, Dior, Dáin.

3 Michel Delving, Bree, Tuckborough, Willowbottom, Hobbiton.

4 Sméagol, Déagol, Bullroarer Took, Bungo, Elros.

5 'No Stone Unturned', 'Roast Mutton', 'On the Doorstep', 'Flies and Spiders', 'A Short Rest'.

6 Fëanor, Aegnor, Aredhel, Glóredhel, Fingon.

7 Gothmog, Galadriel, Melian, Sauron, Mithrandir.

8 Khazad-dûm, Gamil Zirak, Kheled-zâram, Zirak-zigil, Kibil-nâla.

9 Incánus, The Grey Pilgrim, Daeron, Láthspell, Tharkûn.

10 Gaffer Gamgee, Farmer Maggot, Farmer Giles of Ham, Tom Bombadil, Beorn.

TIE BREAK

◆ Which of the following did not lose any hands, feet or fingers? Beren, Maglor, Maedhros, Morgoth, Frodo, Gelmir.

STARTER

◆ Why was Wootton Major so called?

1 How often did the Feast of Good Children come around?

2 What was the Master Cook's most important duty at this feast?

3 What were the names of the Master Cook and his apprentice?

4 When the fay-star fell out of Smith's mouth, what did he do with it?

5 What was the name of Smith's wife?

6 From what sea did the elven mariners disembark?

7 What happened when Smith stepped onto the fiery red lake?

8 What did his wife find in his hair?

9 Where had Smith seen the Queen of Faery before?

10 What was special about Alf and what choice did he give to Smith?

TIE BREAK

◆ Nokes's closing remark dismissed Alf as too what, you might say?

85 · SAURON

STARTER

◆ Why was Frodo of great importance to Sauron?

1 In the beginning, Sauron was one of the Maiar of which Vala?

2 What does the Quenya 'Sauron' mean in English?

3 Melkor assigned to Sauron the command of which great underground fortress?

4 Which King of Númenor did Sauron corrupt to the worship of Melkor?

5 What was the name of Sauron's stronghold in Mirkwood, and by what name was he known there?

6 What was the emblem of Sauron in Mordor?

7 Who were Sauron's most trusted servants?

8 Who called Sauron 'the Black Hand'?

9 What was the name of Sauron's tower in Mordor?

10 What happened to the creatures of Sauron after the destruction of the One Ring?

TIE BREAK

◆ Why did Sauron's temple dome in Númenor turn black?

86 · GIMLI

STARTER

◆ Where did Frodo first see Gimli?

1 Who was Gimli's father?

2 What was Gimli's preferred weapon?

3 Where had Gimli travelled from to be at the Council of Elrond?

4 Why did he linger in the Chamber of Mazarbul?

5 What gift did he ask of Galadriel?

6 Who did Gimli mistake for Saruman?

7 Given a year and a hundred of his kind, what could Gimli have made of Helm's Deep?

8 How many foes did he slay in the Battle of the Hornburg?

9 What did Gimli's people forge for Minas Tirith?

10 After the death of Elessar, what happened to Gimli?

TIE BREAK

◆ Which wind did Aragorn and Legolas leave Gimli to sing of, and what was his response?

STARTER

◆ What did many goblins ride at the Battle of Five Armies?

1 Who or what were the Valaraukar?

2 What did Boromir do to arouse the Watcher in the Water?

3 What island was renamed Tol-in-Gaurhoth, and what did it mean?

4 In Hobbit lore what sort of creature was Fastitocalon?

5 Who helped Melkor to destroy the Two Trees of Valinor?

6 What was the source of the fire of the Balrogs?

7 Where did the Phial of Galadriel become 'A light when all other lights go out'?

8 What prophecy did Melkor breed the great wolf Carharoth to fulfil?

9 Who were eating mutton when Thorin's Company came upon them?

10 What sort of creatures were the Mewlips supposed to be?

TIE BREAK

◆ Who fatally wounded Fëanor after Dagor-nuin-Giliath?

88 · LÓRIEN

STARTER

◆ What kind of place in Middle-earth was Lórien?

1 Who founded Lórien?

2 What was the chief city of Lórien?

3 What name did the Rohirrim give to Lórien?

4 Lórien was protected from Sauron by the power of which ring?

5 What was the Sindarin name for the Silverlode?

6 What trees were peculiar to Lórien?

7 Who was the daughter of Celeborn and Galadriel, and whom did she marry?

8 Who was the brother of Rúmil and Orophin?

9 What colour was Celeborn's hair?

10 Who did Frodo see climbing up his tree in Lórien?

TIE BREAK

◆ In the War of the Ring, Lórien was attacked three times from where?

STARTER

> ◆ Which book provides the overall structure of Tolkien's mythos?

1 What was the first story from *The Silmarillion* to be put on paper?

2 On what European languages were Quenya and Sindarin respectively based?

3 Which major character in *The Silmarillion* was inspired by Edith Tolkien?

4 The legend of Númenor had its origins in what nightmare?

5 What county in particular was The Shire modelled on?

6 Tolkien lifted all the dwarf-names in *The Hobbit* from what ancient literary work?

7 Which character started out as a hobbit called 'Trotter'?

8 Whose voice was Treebeard's way of speaking based on?

9 *The Lord of the Rings* is properly divided into how many books?

10 Who helped Tolkien by drawing an elaborate map of Middle-earth?

TIE BREAK

> ◆ What did Tolkien initially call the sea-voyager in *The Book of Lost Tales*?

STARTER

◆ What was most precious to Gollum?

1 What were the Seven Hoards?

2 Who threw his Silmaril into the Sea?

3 For whom did the Dwarves make the Nauglamír?

4 What treasure did Bilbo take home from Smaug's hoard?

5 Who gave the Old Took a pair of magic diamond studs?

6 From whom did Sauron take the last Ring of the Dwarves?

7 What did Tom Bombadil take for himself from the Barrow-Wight's treasures?

8 Who gave Vilya to Elrond?

9 Describe the White Crown which Gandalf set upon Aragorn's head.

10 Who did Elessar give the Star of the Dúnedain to?

TIE BREAK

◆ Why was Frodo reluctant for Aragorn to look at his wound from the Chamber of Mazarbul?

91 · THE LETTER 'E'

STARTER

◆ I'm about fourteen feet tall and look like a cross between a Man and a tree. What am I?

All the answers to the following begin with the letter 'E':

1 What kind of creature was called 'thoron' in Sindarin?

2 Who was the only Sinda to have seen the Two Trees?

3 The palantír which looked to the Undying Lands was kept where?

4 Name the Peredhil.

5 What kind of beings were Finglas and Fladrif?

6 Aragorn was known by this name in his youth.

7 Give the Sindarin name for the Tower Hills.

8 The valley of Tumladen lay in the midst of which mountains?

9 Aragorn, disguised as Thorongil, served Gondor during whose Stewardship?

10 Who was the father of Isildur and Anárion?

TIE BREAK

◆ Where did the King of the Mountains swear allegiance to Isildur?

STARTER

◆ In what forest did Tom Bombadil live?

1 What name did the Dwarves give to Tom?

2 Who was Tom's wife, and who was her mother?

3 What colour were his boots?

4 In 'Bombadil Goes Boating', how did he come by the blue feather in his hat?

5 Who wrote the poem 'The Stone Troll'?

6 What was he carrying when Frodo and Sam found him?

7 To whom did he say, 'Eat earth! Dig deep! Drink water! Go to sleep!'?

8 When Frodo asked Goldberry, 'Who is Tom Bombadil?' what was her reply?

9 What was the name of Tom's pony?

10 What did Tom bid lie 'free to all finders'?

TIE BREAK

◆ Why would it have been unwise to entrust the Ring to Bombadil?

93 · THE WAR OF THE RING – II

STARTER

◆ Who died defending Merry and Pippin against Orcs?

1 Who carried Gandalf from the peak of Zirak-zigil after his fight with the Balrog?

2 Why did Merry and Pippin have reason to thank Grishnákh?

3 Which members of the Fellowship were besieged in the Battle of the Hornburg?

4 Isengard was destroyed by whom?

5 Who was the Captain of the Tower of Cirith Ungol when Frodo was imprisoned there?

6 Who commanded the men of Dol Amroth at the Battle of the Pelennor Fields?

7 Who helped Aragorn to defeat the Corsairs at Pelargir?

8 Where did the hobbits find a barrier with a large board saying NO ROAD?

9 What title was given to Gimli after the War of the Ring?

10 On Frodo's return to the Shire, who had become known as the Chief?

TIE BREAK

◆ Which of Faramir's Rangers asked for permission to shoot Gollum?

STARTER

◆ They were called the Firstborn, the Elder People, the Fair Folk and the Folk of the Wood. Who were they?

Match each generic or racial name with its equivalent:

1 Gonnhirrim	A. Ents
2 Gorgûn	B. Golodhrim
3 Onodrim	C. Hobbits
4 Helmingas	D. Númenóreans
5 Periannath	E. Sea-elves
6 Noldor	F. Dwarves
7 Teleri	G. Yrch
8 Noegyth Nibin	H. Rohirrim
9 Dúnedain	I. Nazgûl
10 Úlairi	J. Petty-dwarves

TIE BREAK

◆ They were called the Apanónar, the Engwar and the Strangers. Who were they?

95 · MELKOR

1 What did Melkor seek in the Void?

2 What other name did the Elves give to Melkor, and what did it mean?

3 When the Elves awoke, Melkor sought to make them fearful of which particular Vala?

4 For how many Ages was Melkor imprisoned in Valinor?

5 Who helped him to despoil the Two Trees and steal away the Silmarils?

6 What injury did the Silmarils inflict on him?

7 Which Lord of the Eagles inflicted great wounds on Melkor?

8 What was the name of Melkor's great mace?

9 What deed of his was held to be the most hateful to Ilúvatar?

10 After the War of Wrath, what was Melkor's fate?

96 · AKALLABÊTH

◆ In the Second Age the Dúnedain dwelt on what island?

1 Name the great central peak of Númenor.

2 Who was the first King of the Dúnedain?

3 What arts did the Dúnedain prize above all others?

4 What did the Valar forbid the Dúnedain to do?

5 Who were the Elendili?

6 What was the chief dwelling of the Faithful in the later days?

7 Who was the mightiest and proudest of all the Kings of Númenor?

8 Why was Sauron brought to Númenor?

9 After the Downfall of Númenor, what ability did Sauron lose?

10 What happened to Valinor and Eressëa when Ilúvatar changed the fashion of the World?

TIE BREAK

◆ Whom did the Dúnedain teach to sow seed, grind grain, hew wood and shape stone?

97 · BOROMIR AND FARAMIR

1 Who was Boromir's father?

2 What gift did Boromir receive from the Lady Galadriel?

3 On what hill did Boromir try to take the Ring from Frodo?

4 How did he vainly try to summon help before he was killed?

5 Which members of the Fellowship did Boromir die defending?

6 What did Aragorn, Legolas and Gimli do to his body in place of burial?

7 What force did Faramir command when Frodo and Sam first met him?

8 Who tried to cremate Faramir while he still lived?

9 When Faramir surrendered his office of Steward to Aragorn, how did Aragorn react?

10 Whom did Faramir marry?

TIE BREAK
◆ Who did Faramir imply were not 'wondrous fair to look upon'?

STARTER

◆ 'Almost felt you liked the Forest! That's good!' Who was Treebeard replying to?

1 Name two rivers that flowed through Fangorn.

2 How many toes did Treebeard have on each foot?

3 What colours were his eyes?

4 Who suggested that Treebeard make a new line for the lore of Living Creatures?

5 How did Treebeard illuminate the inside of Wellinghall?

6 What name was given to the region where the gardens of the Entwives had once been?

7 What was an Entmoot?

8 What was Quickbeam's Elvish name?

9 How did Beechbone die?

10 Who summoned the Ents and Huorns to the Battle of the Hornburg?

TIE BREAK

◆ In the lore of Living Creatures, hawk was the swiftest and swan the whitest. What was the coldest?

99 · THE ROHIRRIM

1 What was the capital of Rohan?

2 What was the name of the great feast-hall therein?

3 From what steed of Valinor were the *Mearas*, the greatest horses of Rohan, said to be descended?

4 What was the usual hair-colour of the Rohirrim, and what name did the Dunlendings give them as a result?

5 Who was the first King of Rohan?

6 At what battle did Eorl and his riders come to aid the army of Gondor against Balchoth and Orcs?

7 Whose words had turned King Théoden into a wizened old man?

8 What gift did Gandalf ask of Théoden?

9 Whose arrival changed the course of the Battle of Helm's Deep?

10 Who led the Rohirrim through Druadan Forest?

TIE BREAK

◆ What standard did Théoden fell at the Battle of the Pelennor Fields?

100 · THE LAST STAGE

1 With what chain was Morgoth bound after the War of Wrath?

2 After the Battle of Five Armies, whom did Dáin crown with gold?

3 To whom did Bard give the emeralds of Girion?

4 Why was Númenor remembered as Mar-nu-Falmar?

5 To whom did Elessar give the Forest of Drúadan for ever?

6 How did Gimli claim a victory over Legolas in a contest of words?

7 Who gave Bill Ferny a kick as he fled from the Brandywine Gate?

8 What office had Robin Smallburrow been appointed to under the Chief?

9 Who were the only two surviving Ring-bearers not to sail West with Gandalf?

10 Whose age did Bilbo pass on the day he departed from the Grey Havens?

TIE BREAK

◆ What was the last sign of Frodo that Sam, Merry and Pippin saw as he sailed away into the West?

ANSWERS:

Quiz · 1

STARTER Gollum

1 The Lamps of the Valar
2 Arien and Tilion
3 The dews of Telperion and Laurelin, the Two Trees of Valinor
4 By using the Phial of Galadriel
5 Gandalf
6 The keyhole of the secret door of Erebor
7 Eärendil
8 Varda
9 The Elves who never saw the Light of the Trees of Valinor
10 Minas Tirith; Lampwrights' Street

TIE BREAK Tirion

Quiz · 2

STARTER Four (Frodo, Sam, Merry and Pippin)

1 Belladonna Took
2 Merry and Pippin
3 The Harfoots, the Fallohides and the Stoors
4 Tobold Hornblower
5 Periannath
6 Déagol
7 In the upper vales of Anduin, between Greenwood the Great and the Misty Mountains
8 Yellow and green
9 The Tooks
10 Merry

TIE BREAK Three (Frodo, Sam and Gollum)

QUIZ · 3

STARTER Bag End

1 The Old Took
2 'Good morning'
3 11 a.m.
4 Hoot like an owl
5 Because it shone when goblins were near
6 'Give me more time! Give me time!'
7 A boat
8 Bard
9 That his belongings were being auctioned off
10 'Translations from the Elvish'

TIE BREAK The Undying Lands (Eressëa)

QUIZ · 4

STARTER Twenty

1 Eleventy-one
2 Five
3 Three: Grip, Fang and Wolf
4 Balin, Ori and Óin
5 Fourteen
6 Treebeard
7 Twenty-sixth
8 The goblins of the Misty Mountains
9 Seven
10 Minas Ithil, Minas Anor, Orthanc, Osgiliath, Elostirion, Annúminas, Amon Sûl

TIE BREAK (The Battle of) Unnumbered Tears

Quiz • 5

STARTER Hobbits

1 The Brandywine
2 The Three-Farthing Stone
3 The Battle of Greenfields
4 Michel Delving
5 Four (North, South, East and West)
6 'The Green Dragon' (in Bywater), 'The Floating Log' (in
   Frogmorton), 'The Ivy Bush' (on Bywater Road) and the
   'Golden Perch' (in Stock)
7 Overhill
8 White Wolves crossed into the Shire
9 The Tooks
10 The Shirriffs

TIE BREAK The Battle of Bywater

Quiz • 6

STARTER The Lonely Mountain, Erebor

1 His pardon
2 Thorin
3 Balin
4 In the trolls' cave
5 That there were moon-letters on it
6 His nice brass buttons
7 He let him stand on his back to climb into a pine tree
8 To meet the goblins of the Misty Mountains
9 He was a skin-changer
10 By hiding in barrels and floating out on the Forest River

TIE BREAK Thorin (after the journey by barrels)

QUIZ • 7

STARTER Esgaroth, Lake-town

1 They rejoiced and sang songs all day
2 The River Running
3 Late autumn, the waning of the year
4 The last light of the setting sun revealed the keyhole
5 A great two-handled cup
6 He shot an arrow into the bare patch in Smaug's left breast; the great thrush whispered in his ear
7 He was a great raven, son of Carc
8 Bolg of the North
9 Dáin son of Náin
10 Gandalf and Balin

TIE BREAK The Elves of Rivendell

QUIZ • 8

STARTER Bilbo

1 Thorin
2 Gandalf
3 Melkor
4 Gandalf
5 Bilbo
6 Treebeard
7 Smaug
8 Strider
9 Gandalf
10 Sam

TIE BREAK Sauron

QUIZ · 9

STARTER North-South

1 The Hithaeglir
2 Fili and Kili
3 Dori
4 Carn Dûm
5 The Witch-king of Angmar
6 Caradhras, Celebdil and Fanuidhol
7 Azanulbizar; Kheled-zâram
8 Holly trees
9 The Silverlode
10 The White Mountains

TIE BREAK Dolmed

QUIZ · 10

STARTER Stone

1 Aulë
2 Belegost and Nogrod in the Blue Mountains, and Khazad-dûm in the Misty Mountains
3 The Grey-elves; 'Masters of stone'
4 Telchar
5 Menegroth, the Thousand Caves
6 'The Necklace of the Dwarves', made for Finrod Felagund
7 Thráin I
8 The Battle of Azanulbizar
9 Dáin II (Dáin Ironfoot)
10 Gimli; it was said that he was allowed to sail over the Sea to the Undying Lands

TIE BREAK The Noldor

QUIZ · 11

STARTER Moonlight

1 The Sea of Nûrnen
2 Tolfalas
3 Fornost in the North Downs
4 The Ephel Dúath (The Mountains of Shadow)
5 The Entwash
6 Angmar
7 Mount Mindolluin
8 The River Lhûn (Lune)
9 The Iron Hills
10 Doriath

TIE BREAK Vinyamar

QUIZ · 12

STARTER Roast mutton

1 Folca of the Rohirrim
2 Nahar
3 Kingsfoil – in the hands of the heirs of Elendil it had great healing powers
4 Any five from the following: Sharp-ears, Wise-nose, Swish-tail, Bumpkin, White-socks.
5 Huan
6 Elanor
7 Snowmane, his mount, fell on him and crushed him
8 Yavanna
9 A daisy on the grass
10 Like a great white swan

TIE BREAK Crebain

Quiz • 13

STARTER Three

1 The stars of heaven
2 Varda
3 The Vanyar, the Noldor and the Teleri
4 Elwë Singollo (Thingol)
5 Fëanor
6 Because they slew many of the Teleri, their own Elven kin
7 Gondolin
8 Elrond and Elros, the Half-elven, who were allowed to choose whether to be joined to the Fate of Elves or of Men
9 At the Grey Havens
10 Their power and glory faded, and eventually almost all the Elves still in Middle-earth departed for the Undying Lands

TIE BREAK Glorfindel's

Quiz • 14

STARTER On a chain around his neck

1 Drogo Baggins
2 Mr Underhill
3 By singing a verse that Tom had taught him
4 The Underhills of Staddle
5 Bilbo
6 He was wearing a coat of mithril-mail
7 A terrible roving Eye
8 A Phial containing the light of Eärendil's star
9 By singing a song that was answered by Frodo
10 The anniversary of the knife-wound of the Nazgûl Lord (October the sixth)

TIE BREAK Snaga

QUIZ · 15

STARTER That goblins/Orcs were nearby

1 C
2 G
3 B
4 D
5 A
6 H
7 E
8 F
9 J
10 I

TIE BREAK The Elves of Nargothrond

QUIZ · 16

STARTER They 'fastened themselves and never came undone till ordered'

1 His skill with fires, smokes and lights
2 Narya
3 Olórin
4 Glamdring
5 He cast it into the fireplace and read the fiery script thus revealed
6 He was carried away by Gwaihir the Windlord
7 Shadowfax
8 He was now arrayed all in white instead of in grey
9 The Ents and Huorns of Fangorn Forest
10 'I will not say: do not weep; for not all tears are an evil'

TIE BREAK Dol Guldur; the identity of its Lord

QUIZ · 17

STARTER None (it was round)

1 Menegroth
2 It was almost entirely built on stilts over the Long Lake
3 The Chamber of Mazarbul
4 In the parlour
5 Green
6 Talan
7 Narvi
8 The Rammas Echor
9 The Tower Hall or the Hall of the Kings in Minas Tirith
10 The 'Chambers of Fire' in Orodruin

TIE BREAK Ilmarin

QUIZ · 18

STARTER Thorin Oakenshield

1 H. Uncle and niece
2 D. Father and son
3 E. Husband and wife
4 A. Brothers
5 J. Uncle and nephew
6 C. Son and father
7 I. Husband and wife
8 B. Grandson and grandfather
9 F. Father and son
10 G. Son and father

TIE BREAK Lúthien and Beren

Quiz · 19

STARTER A Professor

1 Bloemfontein in the Orange Free State in 1892
2 She converted to Catholicism
3 King Edward's School, Birmingham
4 Sarehole
5 The Tea Club/Barrovian Society at King Edward's
6 Father Francis Morgan
7 Classics
8 Eärendil
9 Signalling
10 He was marking examination papers and wrote it on a blank page

TIE BREAK By seeing it on the sides of coal-trucks

Quiz · 20

STARTER Frodo

1 Taniquetil and Oiolossë
2 Because he had healed their lord from an arrow-wound
3 Maedhros
4 Five feet high
5 Eöl
6 Aragorn, Legolas and Gimli
7 Beorn
8 Amon Rûdh
9 Red
10 Any three from: Gwaihir, Landroval, Thorondor and Meneldor

TIE BREAK To hinder the riding of Oromë

QUIZ · 21

STARTER His ring finger

1 Ulmo
2 Maedhros
3 Utumno
4 The blade of his knife Angrist snapped
5 Gollum
6 Frodo
7 Uinen
8 The Valaraukar
9 The Arkenstone of Thráin
10 Pippin

TIE BREAK The Dwarf-city of Nogrod

QUIZ · 22

STARTER Rivendell

1 King Thranduil of Mirkwood
2 Faggots of wood
3 September
4 Orcs
5 Beorn's
6 Gandalf
7 What was left of the dust given to him by Galadriel
8 William the Troll's
9 A ferocious kind of winged insect
10 Gríma Wormtongue

TIE BREAK Húrin

QUIZ · 23

STARTER Gandalf

1 D
2 I
3 A
4 H
5 C
6 B
7 J
8 F
9 G
10 E

TIE BREAK Maeglin

QUIZ · 24

STARTER The Wizards (Istari)

1 Manwë
2 Lord of the Breath of Arda
3 Elbereth
4 Ulmo
5 Yavanna; Aulë
6 Mandos; he was the Keeper of the Houses of the Dead
7 Lórien; to find rest and the easing of their burdens
8 Nienna
9 Tulkas; wrestling and contests of strength
10 Oromë

TIE BREAK Ulmo

QUIZ · 25

STARTER Hobbiton

1 A gardener
2 He caught him eavesdropping
3 To see Elves
4 Making a fire
5 Bill the pony
6 In the Mirror of Galadriel
7 Gollum writhed and screamed in pain
8 When he overheard Shagrat saying so
9 In the Party Field; it grew into a mallorn tree
10 Seven

TIE BREAK Because he had been a Ring-bearer

QUIZ · 26

STARTER Gollum

1 Isildur
2 It slipped from his finger as he swam the Anduin, and Orcs killed him with arrows
3 Because he began his ownership of the Ring with Pity
4 Because he was about to put it on and draw off the giant spiders of Mirkwood
5 For avoiding unpleasant callers
6 He put it in his pocket instead
7 Elvish script and Black Speech of Mordor
8 Tom Bombadil
9 Boromir
10 When Frodo put on the Ring in Mount Doom

TIE BREAK The Gladden Fields

Quiz · 27

STARTER Thorin Oakenshield

1 The Uruk-hai
2 A bow
3 Maglor
4 Saruman's Orcs
5 Faramir
6 The Battle of the Gladden Fields
7 A Moon disfigured by a death's head
8 Goblins, Wolves, Elves, Men and Dwarves
9 A fighting-force of Rohan (exclusively cavalry?)
10 The Battle of the Field of Celebrant

TIE BREAK In a fight between his company and a Minas Morgul troop over Frodo's mithril-mail

Quiz · 28

STARTER Hobbiton

1 Minas Tirith
2 The Gamgees
3 Túna
4 The museum in Michel Delving
5 Seven
6 Westfarthing
7 The Tower of the Moon
8 Armenelos
9 Deadmen's Dike
10 Osgiliath

TIE BREAK Demolishing its great stone bridge

Quiz • 29

STARTER Gimli

1 Melian – not a mountain (a Maia, wife of Thingol)
2 Brodda – not a beast/monster (an Easterling)
3 Gollum – not a member of the Fellowship
4 Tol Galen – not an original location of a palantír (an island in the river Adurant)
5 Maeglin – not a son of Fëanor (son of Eöl and Aredhel)
6 Vanyar – the only group of Elves to go to Aman
7 falas – not a colour (a shore, a line of surf)
8 Uglúk – not a servant of Sauron (an Uruk-hai of Isengard)
9 Grond – not a sword (the great mace of Morgoth)
10 The Tower Hills – not mentioned as the site of a battle

TIE BREAK Dior

Quiz • 30

STARTER False

1 A hobbit
2 Trahald or Sméagol
3 Thin and wiry with large hands and large webbed feet, and bulging pale eyes
4 Six
5 His precious
6 It was his 'birthday present'
7 Fish and goblin-flesh
8 Aragorn
9 Legolas
10 Slinker and Stinker

TIE BREAK Lembas

QUIZ · 31

STARTER Tree

1 Mr Parish
2 To fetch the doctor and the builder for Parish
3 To make repairs on Parish's house
4 The merits and faults of his past life
5 He put some salve on them which healed them at once
6 His bicycle
7 Because he had come upon his Tree
8 Towards the Mountains
9 In the Town Museum
10 They both laughed

TIE BREAK 'On Fairy-Stories'

QUIZ · 32

STARTER (d)

1 (d)
2 (b)
3 (a)
4 (d)
5 (c)
6 (a)
7 (e)
8 (b)
9 (e)
10 (a)

TIE BREAK (c)

QUIZ · 33

STARTER Gimli

1 F
2 J
3 A
4 B
5 C
6 D
7 H
8 G
9 I
10 E

TIE BREAK Mîm the Petty-Dwarf

QUIZ · 34

STARTER A Ranger

1 Strider
2 Narsil and Andúril
3 Thorongil
4 In Rivendell
5 Athelas
6 That all the Company be blindfolded
7 Galadriel
8 Wingfoot
9 The Dead Men of Dunharrow
10 Gandalf; Arwen

TIE BREAK To be King of both Arnor and Gondor

Quiz · 35

STARTER *The Fellowship of the Ring, The Two Towers* and *The Return of the King*

1 Round
2 Gandalf
3 The Long Lake
4 The Great Eagles
5 Bree
6 Nine
7 Rivendell
8 Thorin Oakenshield
9 To the Cracks of Doom in Orodruin (Mount Doom)
10 The Battle of the Pelennor Fields

TIE BREAK Hobbits

Quiz · 36

STARTER Lovers

1 Thingol and Melian
2 Into the Hidden Kingdom of Doriath
3 Tinúviel; 'Nightingale'
4 Daeron
5 That he would neither slay Beren nor imprison him
6 Because he held aloft the ring of Felagund
7 Huan
8 Curufin
9 Carcharoth bit off his right hand containing the Silmaril (Erchamion means 'One-handed')
10 She alone of the Elves was accounted among Men

TIE BREAK Barahir's hand, wearing the ring of Finrod Felagund

QUIZ · 37

STARTER An innkeeper
1 Háma
2 Bill Ferny
3 Bucklebury
4 They were cousins
5 Barad-dûr, Isengard and the Misty Mountains
6 He was after mushrooms
7 An Elf of Lothlórien
8 Túrin Turambar
9 Because he never answered letters
10 Elanor

TIE BREAK The Ivy Bush

QUIZ · 38

STARTER *The Lord of the Rings*
1 'The Passing of the Grey Company'
2 'Riddles in the Dark'
3 'The Road to Isengard'
4 'The Shadow of the Past'
5 'Of the Rings of Power and the Third Age'
6 'At the Sign of *The Prancing Pony*'
7 'Fire and Water'
8 'The Field of Cormallen'
9 'Of the Silmarils and the Unrest of the Noldor'
10 'An Unexpected Party'

TIE BREAK 'Mount Doom'

QUIZ · 39

STARTER Gollum

1 Longbottom
2 Indis
3 Amon Sûl
4 The Lockholes
5 The Esgalduin
6 Aiglos (or Aeglos)
7 Gorgûn
8 Dáin II Ironfoot
9 Rúmil
10 Galadriel

TIE BREAK Tuor

QUIZ · 40

STARTER Half-true

1 G
2 B
3 E
4 I
5 C
6 J
7 D
8 F
9 A
10 H

TIE BREAK The Swans

QUIZ · 41

1 33
2 Pippin
3 Gildor Inglorion
4 Old Man Willow
5 He slipped on the Ring and vanished
6 'O Elbereth! Gilthoniel!'
7 Their way was blocked by a terrible blizzard
8 Mellon
9 Two pale points of light like eyes
10 Gimli

TIE BREAK The Brown Lands

QUIZ · 42

STARTER Men

1 Pelargir, Dol Amroth, Minas Ithil, Minas Anor and Osgiliath, the capital
2 Minas Ithil fell to the Nazgûl
3 A white tree, a silver crown and seven stars on a black field
4 Seven
5 From: Lossarnach, Ringló Vale, Morthond, the Anfalas (Langstrand), Lamedon, the Ethir, Pinnath Gelin, Dol Amroth
6 Pippin
7 Minas Anor; the 'Tower of the Sun'
8 Because their leader, Faramir, was Boromir's brother
9 The Rohirrim
10 A palantír

TIE BREAK Harondor

Quiz · 43

STARTER Mutton

1 Gollum
2 A type of thin cake, or waybread, that Elves baked to sustain travellers on long journeys
3 Beorn
4 Barliman Butterbur's
5 Mushrooms
6 Because it used to brew the best beer in the Eastfarthing
7 Because they had drunk of the ent-draughts
8 Fish
9 Fili
10 Ungoliant

TIE BREAK Bombur

Quiz · 44

STARTER Buckland

1 Kalimac
2 Nob
3 Uglúk
4 Sitting and smoking
5 King Théoden's
6 A pony of Rohan, given to Merry by Théoden
7 By stabbing the knee of the Nazgûl Lord and diverting the blow of his mace
8 A silver horn
9 Estella Bolger
10 From: 'Herblore of the Shire', 'Reckoning of Years' and 'Old Words and Names in the Shire'

TIE BREAK By drinking ent-draughts

QUIZ · 45

STARTER In the Misty Mountains

1 By capturing and torturing Elves
2 Black (also decribed as 'sallow')
3 In the valley of the River Gelion
4 Dagor Bragollach, the Battle of Sudden Flame
5 The Uruk-hai
6 Gundabad
7 Azog
8 Gandalf
9 Minas Morgul
10 A lesser, weaker breed of Orc; 'slave'

TIE BREAK Andúril

QUIZ · 46

STARTER A Wizard (Istar) or Maia

1 Curunír; 'Man of Skill'
2 Ring-lore
3 So that the One Ring might reveal itself
4 Through the palantír of Orthanc
5 A white S-rune
6 Gríma Wormtongue
7 Garments of many colours
8 The Orkish *sharkû* or 'old man'
9 Radagast
10 A misty figure rose from the body but was blown away; the body itself shrank and shrivelled

TIE BREAK King's jester

QUIZ · 47

STARTER Thorin's Company

1 Sam
2 Beren
3 Thorin's Company
4 Frodo
5 Bilbo
6 Legolas
7 A Barrow-wight
8 Sam
9 The Elves of Rivendell
10 Treebeard (or the Ents)

TIE BREAK Sauron

QUIZ · 48

STARTER The 19th

1 G
2 D
3 C
4 F
5 A
6 I
7 J
8 E
9 B
10 H

TIE BREAK Leeds University

QUIZ • 49

STARTER Mordor

1 The Tower of Avallóne
2 The Tower of Cirith Ungol
3 Unbreakable stone
4 Minas Anor and Minas Ithil
5 Narchost and Carchost
6 Elostirion
7 Finrod, in the Falas west of Eglarest
8 Because the One Ring still survived
9 White
10 Barad Eithel

TIE BREAK Gondolin

QUIZ • 50

STARTER Britain

1 Ægidius Ahenobarbus Julius Agricola de Hammo
2 Garm
3 Old nails and bits of wire, pieces of broken pot, bones and stones and other rubbish
4 He thought he had been stung by some fierce insect
5 A letter of approbation and a sword
6 A Mock Dragon's Tail made of confectionery
7 Chrysophylax Dives
8 Caudimordax
9 The parson
10 The Wormwardens

TIE BREAK Gloom

QUIZ • 51

STARTER Thorin & Co.

1 Beorn
2 Bilbo
3 Boromir
4 Bilbo
5 Gandalf
6 Smaug
7 Théoden
8 Éomer
9 Dori
10 Gimli

TIE BREAK Faramir

QUIZ • 52

STARTER 'Flies and Spiders'

1 Rhovanion; Wilderland
2 Greenwood the Great
3 Dol Guldur
4 Thranduil
5 Because it carried enchantment and a great drowsiness and forgetfulness
6 Horrible pale bulbous eyes, 'Insect eyes', as Bilbo thought
7 Bombur
8 Black
9 Sting
10 A crown of berries and red leaves

TIE BREAK It was cleared of evil and renamed Eryn Lasgalen, Wood of Green Leaves

Quiz · 53

STARTER West

1 The Teleri; 'Those of the waves'
2 Ulmo drew them across the sea on an island
3 Ossë
4 Swans
5 Círdan the Shipwright
6 Haven of the Swans
7 Brithombar and Eglarest
8 Ar-Pharazôn's
9 Nine
10 Aragorn and the Dead Men of Dunharrow

TIE BREAK Gondor

Quiz · 54

STARTER Burglar

1 A small flower found in Neldoreth and Lórien
2 He fell through a trapdoor and broke his neck
3 Olog-hai
4 He didn't react when Sam took the Ring from him
5 Troll
6 Eöl
7 Lake Cuiviénen
8 Varda's
9 Leave the path
10 The Westmarch

TIE BREAK A family of hobbits in Bree

QUIZ · 55

1 Sam Gamgee
2 For an animated motion-picture of *The Lord of the Rings*
3 A furore was caused by the publication, in the U.S.A., of a pirate edition of *The Lord of the Rings*
4 A lion, two emus, and a tree bearing bulbous fruit
5 Tolkien, C. S. Lewis and Charles Williams
6 Dick Plotz
7 Warwick University
8 A psychedelic cult magazine
9 William Ready
10 'Dungeons and Dragons'

TIE BREAK S. Gollum

QUIZ · 56

STARTER Yes

1 Peregrin Took
2 Paladin Took
3 He chided him for his foolishness
4 A brooch
5 Bregalad (Quickbeam)
6 He looked into the palantír of Orthanc
7 Denethor
8 Faramir
9 Counsellor of the North-kingdom
10 In Rath Dínen

TIE BREAK Shadowfax

Quiz · 57

STARTER False (it was Durin's Folk)

1 The Dwarrowdelf (Phurunargian)
2 The Dimrill Dale (Azanulbizar or Nanduhirion)
3 A Balrog
4 Balin
5 Celebdil (Zirak-zigil)
6 Mithril
7 Because the Watcher in the Water had blocked it up
8 Because he had slightly mistranslated the inscription on it
9 The House of Fëanor
10 'They are coming'

TIE BREAK None

Quiz · 58

STARTER Smaug

1 The Urulóki (fire-drakes), the winged dragons and the cold drakes
2 Black
3 Glaurung
4 Because he had revealed himself to the world before he had grown to full might
5 The Dwarves of Belegost
6 Gurthang
7 Thorondor and the great birds of heaven and Eärendil in his flying ship 'Vingilot'
8 Scatha the Worm
9 Smaug
10 Bard

TIE BREAK Dagor Bragollach, the Battle of Sudden Flame

QUIZ · 59

STARTER The Valar

1 The Máhanaxar
2 Laurelin and Telperion
3 The Pelóri
4 Ezellohar
5 Valimar (or Valmar)
6 In the Silmarils
7 To pursue to the ends of the World any being or creature that withheld a Silmaril from them
8 They became the Moon and Sun
9 Finarfin
10 The Enchanted Isles

TIE BREAK Oromë and Tulkas

QUIZ · 60

STARTER A large rider wrapped in a black cloak and hood, which concealed his face, on a black horse

1 The Black Speech
2 Nine; they were originally powerful Men, kings, sorcerors, warriors
3 By giving each of them one of the Nine Rings
4 Angmar
5 To prepare the way for Sauron's return to Mordor
6 Minas Morgul; the 'Tower of Sorcery'
7 Five
8 A fragment of the blade was lodged in his shoulder and working its way towards his heart
9 They were swept away by a great flood
10 Éowyn of the Rohirrim

TIE BREAK Fatty Bolger

QUIZ · 61

STARTER From: Bilbo, Frodo, Sam, Merry, Pippin, the Old Took, Fatty Bolger, Gollum

1 Frodo, Sam, Merry, Pippin, Gandalf, Aragorn, Boromir, Legolas and Gimli
2 From: Elanor, Frodo, Rose, Merry, Pippin, Goldilocks, Hamfast, Daisy, Primrose, Bilbo, Ruby, Robin and Tolman
3 Maedhros, Maglor, Celegorm, Caranthir, Curufin, Amrod, Amras
4 Caradhras, Celebdil and Fanuidhol
5 Isildur, Gollum, Bilbo, Frodo and Sam
6 Thorin, Balin, Dwalin, Fili, Kili, Óin, Glóin, Dori, Nori, Ori, Bifur, Bofur, Bombur, Bilbo and Gandalf
7 Manwë and Varda, Ulmo, Yavanna and Aulë, Mandos, Nienna and Oromë
8 Nogrod, Belegost and Moria
9 Vilya, Narya and Nenya
10 Bill, Bert and Tom

TIE BREAK From: the Rohirrim, Lake Men, Bardings, Woodmen, Beornings, Bree-folk, Rangers, Men of Éothéod

QUIZ · 62

STARTER Thorin's Company

1 The Great East Road
2 Imladris
3 Elrond
4 Vilya
5 That there were moon-letters on it
6 The River Loudwater or Bruinen
7 Arwen
8 To seek the meaning of a riddle that came to him in a dream
9 Gandalf
10 That Gollum had escaped from the Elves of Mirkwood

TIE BREAK It had rolled down the Anduin to the Sea, where it would lie until the End

QUIZ · 63

STARTER 'DON'T LEAVE THE PATH!'

1 The Gelion
2 The Harad Road
3 Tharbad
4 The Sirion
5 The North Road
6 The Anduin
7 The Andram
8 The Celebrant or Silverlode
9 The Sea of Rhûn
10 The Grey Havens

TIE BREAK The Carrock

QUIZ · 64

STARTER Lithlad (Sindarin for a plain in Mordor)

1 C
2 F
3 I
4 B
5 A
6 D
7 J
8 G
9 E
10 H

TIE BREAK Gondolin

Quiz · 65

STARTER No, by the Elves

1 A (poisoned) javelin
2 Beater
3 Gurthang
4 The Men of Westernesse
5 A great black mace
6 Beleg Strongbow's
7 Telchar
8 A blade like a stabbing sword of fire and a great many-thonged whip
9 Because his last victim had worn an iron collar
10 He was shot by three hobbit-archers

TIE BREAK With slender bows

Quiz · 66

STARTER Smaug

1 Gandalf
2 Théoden
3 Beorn
4 Strider/Aragorn
5 Lúthien
6 Tom Bombadil
7 Treebeard
8 Bard
9 Glóin
10 Elrond

TIE BREAK Ulmo

Quiz · 67

STARTER you boo!

1 Rayner Unwin
2 *The Times* and *The Times Literary Supplement*
3 C. S. Lewis, Richard Hughes and Naomi Mitchison
4 Peter Green
5 *Theology*
6 W. H. Auden
7 An overwhelmingly enthusiastic one
8 That all the characters were boys masquerading as adults
9 Bernard Levin
10 One of amusement

TIE BREAK *The Times*

Quiz · 68

STARTER None

1 The word meant 'sickly', referring to their frailty of body and spirit
2 Beren
3 Finrod Felagund
4 Because they were hewers of trees and hunters of beasts
5 The House of Bëor, the House of the Haladin and the House of Hador
6 Arnor and Gondor
7 Rangers
8 The Great Plague
9 Beorn
10 Black Númenóreans (Carsairs)

TIE BREAK Annúminas

Quiz • 69

STARTER caverns

1 western lands
2 Théoden; Thengling
3 Oliphaunt
4 birds; firtrees
5 Living Creatures; free peoples
6 Dunharrow
7 Gil-galad
8 Snowmane
9 Eärendil; Arvernien
10 Tomnoddy; Tomnoddy

TIE BREAK mellon (friend)

Quiz • 70

STARTER *The Silmarillion*

1 Six (including the Great Battle)
2 Denethor
3 Almost all of them were slain by the Dwarves of Mount Dolmed
4 Dagor-nuin-Giliath (the Battle-under-Stars), fought in Mithrim
5 He drew ahead of his comrades in pursuit of the fleeing Orcs and rendered himself vulnerable to attack
6 Glaurung
7 Dagor Bragollach, the Battle of Sudden Flame
8 Anfauglith, the Gasping Dust
9 They betrayed the Eldar by going over suddenly to Morgoth
10 The unloosing of the winged dragons

TIE BREAK Fingolfin

QUIZ · 71

STARTER Frodo

1 Ulfang
2 Goldilocks
3 They were brother and sister
4 Indis of the Vanyar
5 One quarter
6 Long Cleeve
7 Hamfast Gamgee (or Ranugad Galbasi/Galpsi)
8 None
9 Thráin and Thrór
10 They were son and mother

TIE BREAK It killed Óin, his uncle

QUIZ · 72

STARTER Gandalf

1 F
2 A
3 H
4 I
5 C
6 B
7 J
8 E
9 D
10 G

TIE BREAK Fingon's

Quiz · 73

1 An employee of Allen and Unwin, she read his unfinished typescript and urged him to complete it
2 C. S. Lewis
3 Bingo Bolger-Baggins
4 Allegory
5 'Leaf by Niggle'
6 Because his son Christopher was training there as an R.A.F. pilot
7 Because they had shown an interest in publishing *The Silmarillion* alongside it
8 Because Tolkien had had great difficulty in finishing the appendices to the story
9 Bernard Levin
10 Beren and Lúthien

TIE BREAK The Tea Club and Barrovian Society (at King Edward's School)

Quiz · 74

STARTER The bow

1 King Thranduil of Mirkwood
2 Leaves
3 Green and brown
4 A bow and a quiver of arrows
5 A Nazgûl on his winged steed
6 Arod
7 In the temporary settlement of Ents and Huorns in Helm's Deep
8 The Glittering Caves of Aglarond
9 Ithilien
10 Gimli

TIE BREAK In Southern Gondor

QUIZ · 75

STARTER Bilbo

1 I
2 D
3 G
4 A
5 E
6 H
7 B
8 J
9 C
10 F

TIE BREAK Húrin

QUIZ · 76

STARTER Wizards

1 (At least) five
2 Maiar, who took the form of old men
3 In the Third Age of Sun
4 Gandalf, Saruman and Radagast (also Alatar and Pallando, and Morinehtar and Rómestámo)
5 Gandalf
6 Brown
7 Rhosgobel in the Vales of Anduin
8 Beren, the Ruling Steward of Gondor
9 The unmaking of the One Ring
10 Gríma Wormtongue

TIE BREAK Galadriel, Elrond and Círdan

QUIZ • 77

STARTER Bilbo, because he put on the Ring

1 Dáin II Ironfoot
2 The Battle of Bywater
3 Bullroarer Took, by knocking off the head of the Orc Golfimbul which sailed down a rabbit-hole
4 Gondor defeated the Wainriders
5 The Battle of the Peak
6 Orodreth and Túrin
7 Gothmog
8 The Battle of Fornost
9 Eorl
10 The Battle of the Five Armies

TIE BREAK To release the winged dragons

QUIZ • 78

STARTER Because it was hidden in the Encircling Mountains

1 Turgon, in the hidden valley of Tumladen
2 Tirion
3 He prophesised that one would come from Nevrast to warn Gondolin in time of peril; by the arms and sword he should be known
4 Images of the Trees of Valinor, wrought by Turgon
5 The Echoriath
6 The Dark Elf; Aredhel
7 The Caragdûr
8 Húrin; the approximate location of Gondolin
9 Because Idril loved Tuor instead of him
10 Ecthelion

TIE BREAK Guarding refugees from Gondolin's fall, he duelled with a Balrog and fell to his death

Quiz · 79

STARTER The Balrog

1 Will Whitfoot
2 15 March TA 3019
3 Esmeralda Took
4 Galathilion
5 Twenty-fourth (twenty-fifth in *Unfinished Tales*)
6 Eöl
7 The Úmanyar
8 The Watcher in the Water took him
9 A substance fashioned by the Elves from mithril
10 A leap-day holiday in the Shire Calendar

TIE BREAK Ghân-buri-Ghân

Quiz · 80

STARTER New Year's Day

1 E
2 D
3 G
4 J
5 H
6 I
7 A
8 C
9 B
10 F

TIE BREAK 2

QUIZ · 81

STARTER Gandalf

1 Black Land
2 The Ered Lithui (Ash Mountains)
3 Udûn
4 The men of Gondor, to prevent any evil from re-entering Mordor
5 Cirith Gorgor (The Haunted Pass)
6 Lugbúrz
7 They were marked with a red eye-shaped blotch on their backs
8 Torech Ungol
9 They took advantage of the confusion as several companies came together
10 'Precious'

TIE BREAK The Nazgûl

QUIZ · 82

STARTER Just over a year

1 Bilbo
2 Aragorn, Legolas and Gimli
3 By crossing the Helcaraxë, the Grinding Ice
4 The Avari, 'The Unwilling'
5 Beren and Lúthien
6 Ulmo's
7 Ten to eleven in the morning
8 Cram
9 Éowyn (Dernhelm)
10 Bilbo, Gandalf, Elrond, Galadriel and Gildor

TIE BREAK To cross the Grinding Ice of the Helcaraxë

Quiz · 83

STARTER Arathorn

1 Manwë – a Vala, not a Maia
2 Dior – not a Dwarf (son of Beren and Lúthien)
3 Bree – not in the Shire
4 Elros – not a Hobbit (brother of Elrond)
5 'No Stone Unturned' – not a chapter in *The Hobbit*
6 Glóredhel – not of the House of Finwë (of the House of Hador) or an Elf
7 Galadriel – an Elf, not a Maia
8 Gamil Zirak – not a Khuzdul place-name (a Dwarf smith)
9 Daeron – not a name given to Gandalf (Thingol's minstrel)
10 Farmer Giles of Ham – not an inhabitant of Middle-earth

TIE BREAK Maglor: Beren and Maedhros lost hands, Morgoth his feet, Frodo his ring finger, and Gelmir hands and feet (and head)

Quiz · 84

STARTER Because it was larger than Wootton Minor

1 Once every twenty-four years
2 To make the Great Cake
3 Nokes and Alf
4 He clapped it to his forehead
5 Nell
6 The Sea of Windless Storm
7 He slipped and fell with a ringing boom and a wild Wind rose up
8 A living flower
9 She had been the fair dancing maid of the Green Vale
10 He was the King of Faery and he let Smith choose which child the star would go to

TIE BREAK Nimble

QUIZ • 85

STARTER Because he bore the One Ring, which Sauron desperately wanted

1 Aulë
2 'Abominable' or 'Abhorred'
3 Angband
4 Ar-Pharazôn
5 Dol Guldur; The Necromancer
6 A red, lidless eye
7 The Nazgûl, or Ringwraiths
8 Gollum
9 Barad-dûr
10 They wandered, witless and purposeless

TIE BREAK Because of the smoke of sacrifices

QUIZ • 86

STARTER At the Council of Elrond (in Rivendell)

1 Glóin
2 An axe
3 The Lonely Mountain
4 Because there stood Balin's tomb
5 A strand of her hair
6 Gandalf
7 A place that armies would have broken upon like water
8 Forty-two
9 Gates of mithril and steel
10 He sailed west to the Undying Lands

TIE BREAK The East Wind: he would say nothing of it

Quiz • 87

STARTER Wargs (great wolves)

1 The Balrogs
2 Boromir threw a stone into the pool
3 Tol Sirion; 'Isle of Werewolves'
4 A gigantic turtle (or 'turtle-fish')
5 Ungoliant
6 Udûn
7 In Shelob's Lair in Cirith Ungol
8 That Huan, the hound of Valinor, would only meet death when he met the mightiest wolf that would ever walk the world
9 The three Trolls (Bert, Tom and William)
10 Evil swamp-dwelling spirits who attacked and killed wayfarers

TIE BREAK Gothmog, Lord of Balrogs

Quiz • 88

STARTER A forest-kingdom of the Elves

1 The Nandorin Elves
2 Caras Galadon
3 Dwimordene
4 Nenya
5 Celebrant
6 Mellyrn (mallorn)
7 Celebrian; Elrond
8 Haldir
9 Silver
10 Gollum

TIE BREAK Dol Guldur

QUIZ · 89

STARTER *The Silmarillion*

1 The Fall of Gondolin
2 Finnish and Welsh
3 Lúthien
4 An Atlantean vision of a vast wave towering over the land
5 Worcestershire
6 The Elder Edda
7 Strider
8 C. S. Lewis's
9 Six
10 His son Christopher

TIE BREAK Eriol

QUIZ · 90

STARTER The One Ring

1 The treasures of the seven Dwarf Fathers
2 Maglor
3 Finrod
4 Two small chests, one filled with silver and the other with gold
5 Gandalf
6 Thráin
7 A brooch set with blue stones
8 Gil-galad
9 A white helm with wings of pearl and silver like those of a sea-bird, set with seven gems of adamant and on its summit a single jewel
10 Sam Gamgee

TIE BREAK Because he didn't want to reveal his wonderful mithril-coat

Quiz • 91

STARTER An Ent

1 Eagle
2 Elwë (Thingol)
3 In Elostirion
4 Elrond and Elros
5 Ents
6 Estel
7 The Emyn Beraid
8 The Echoriath or Encircling Mountains
9 Ecthelion II
10 Elendil

TIE BREAK At the Stone of Erech (on the Hill of Erech)

Quiz • 92

STARTER The Old Forest

1 Forn
2 Goldberry, daughter of the River-woman
3 Yellow
4 The King's fisher dropped it down and he caught it
5 Sam Gamgee
6 A pile of water-lilies
7 Old Man Willow
8 'He is'
9 Fatty Lumpkin
10 The treasures of the Barrow-mound

TIE BREAK Because it meant so little to him that he would have been dangerously careless with it

QUIZ · 93

STARTER Boromir

1 Gwaihir
2 Because he carried them to safety when the Rohirrim slaughtered his Orc compaions
3 Aragorn, Legolas and Gimli
4 The Ents
5 Shagrat
6 Prince Imrahil
7 The Dead Men of Dunharrow
8 At Frogmorton
9 Lord of the Glittering Caves
10 Lotho Baggins

TIE BREAK Anborn

QUIZ · 94

STARTER The Elves

1 F
2 G
3 A
4 H
5 C
6 B
7 E
8 J
9 D
10 I

TIE BREAK Men

QUIZ · 95

STARTER First

1 The Imperishable Flame
2 Morgoth, the Dark Enemy (or Black Foe) of the World
3 Oromë
4 Three
5 Ungoliant
6 They burnt his hands
7 Thorondor
8 Grond
9 The breeding of the Orcs
10 To be cast out into the Void

TIE BREAK Pile them into a great mound (Haudh-en-Nirnaeth, the Hill of Tears)

QUIZ · 96

STARTER Númenor

1 Meneltarma
2 Elros (Tar-Minyatur)
3 Ship-building and sea-craft
4 To sail westwards out of sight of Númenor
5 The Elf-friends, those Dúnedain who wished to keep the friendship of the Eldar and the Valar
6 The land around Rómenna
7 Ar-Pharazôn
8 To act as a hostage for himself and his servants in Middle-earth
9 The ability to appear fair to the eyes of Men
10 They were taken from the world into the realm of hidden things

TIE BREAK The Men of Middle-earth

Quiz · 97

STARTER They were brothers

1 Denethor II
2 A belt of gold
3 Amon Hen
4 By blowing on his horn
5 Merry and Pippin
6 They laid it in an elven-boat and let the waters of the Auduin carry it away
7 The Rangers of Ithilien
8 Denethor
9 He declared that the office should continue as long as his line lasted
10 Éowyn

TIE BREAK Frodo and Sam

Quiz · 98

STARTER Pippin

1 The Entwash and the Limlight
2 Seven
3 Brown, shot with a green light
4 Pippin
5 He held his hands over two great vessels, causing them to glow
6 The Brown Lands
7 A gathering of Ents
8 Bregalad
9 He was burnt to death by a spray of liquid fire in Isengard
10 Gandalf

TIE BREAK Serpent

QUIZ · 99

STARTER Horses

1 Edoras
2 Meduseld
3 Nahar
4 Golden; Forgoil or 'Strawheads'
5 Eorl the Young
6 The Battle of the Field of Celebrant
7 Gríma Wormtongue
8 Shadowfax
9 That of Gandalf, the Ents and the Huorns
10 Ghân-buri-Ghân

TIE BREAK The black serpent of the Southrons

QUIZ · 100

STARTER Because he was 'only quite a little fellow in a wide world after all!'

1 Angainor
2 The chief of the Eagles
3 The Elvenking
4 Because it was swallowed up by the sea (the name means 'home-beneath-waves')
5 Ghân-buri-Ghân and his folk
6 Legolas was speechless after seeing the Glittering Caves
7 Bill the pony
8 Shirriff
9 Círdan and Sam
10 That of the Old Took

TIE BREAK The light of the glass of Galadriel